DEADLINE

A Novel by Kristin Sanford

D1737710

Dedicated to my family and friends for their never-ending support, patience, and love.

<u>Prologue</u>

Carrie pushed her chair back from the computer table and stretched her arms out. The birds were singing a morning melody that accented the warmth making its way through the open window.

She stood and began making her way downstairs, her nose following the aroma of freshly-brewed coffee. After pouring a cup, Carrie stepped out onto the wrap-around porch and nestled into the swinging chair that was hanging on one side. The mountains in the distance and the morning sky complete with strokes of orange, purple, and pink running through its blue canvas was the reason she moved here three months ago.

Carrie could remember the day she found the house. She needed to get away from the big city for a while, so she packed up some clothes, threw her bags in the back of her car and headed east toward the Great Smokey Mountains. She really didn't have a destination in mind; she was just going to drive until her gut told her to stop – or until she ran out of gas.

She was approaching Knoxville when she remembered the town of Rugby. A friend in college had told her about this little Victorian hamlet nestled in the hills of northeastern Tennessee, so she consulted her map, got off the interstate, and headed for the village. It was love at first sight. It didn't take her long to find a house within driving distance. It was one of the happiest times in her life.

Carrie ran her hands over the scars on her arms that reminded her of a different time. Though the physical pain that had ravaged her body for so long was now gone, the emotional pain was still a battle. Some days, her mind took control and brought her back to a place she never wanted to experience again. She would hear that voice, feel those hands inflicting damage on her, and she would curl up in a ball on the bed and stay there for hours, or even days.

Some days, she would be taken back to the funeral, and the long goodbye that she still hadn't finished saying, even two years later. She would find herself standing there, looking sadly upon the casket that held her first true love, and would struggle to find an escape back to reality.

She used to question how long she would have to endure this pain. There were days in the past when she even contemplated ending the pain with her own hand – finishing what had been started so long ago. Therapy has taught her that all of those feelings were normal and that she would survive; and for the most part that was true. But there were those days that sent her to the brink of insanity. Those were the days she truly dreaded.

A quick shake of the head brought Carrie back to reality. She walked back into the house, poured a fresh cup of coffee, and walked back to her office. She had been working on her book for a year, and as it was nearing its end, Carrie found the memories were becoming harder and harder to endure. She rubbed her scars once again, and sat behind her computer, ready to finish the story once and for all.

1

If they had been paying attention, they would have noticed the man sitting on the park bench was watching them with sinister eyes. They would have noticed that the newspaper he held had coffee stains and was two weeks old. They would have noticed his gloved hands and covered arms in the middle of July. And they just might have noticed him walking away with the little boy who had wandered from home and was not yet missed.

2

Carrie opened the door to the newsroom and closed her eyes as the icy air hit her sweat-drenched face. The hot July sun made the city feel like a sauna, and she was glad to be indoors. She was regretting her decision to walk the nine blocks from the newsroom to the City Council chambers for the monthly Thursday meeting, but considering the price of gas and the empty tank in her worn-down Mazda, she had no choice.

"Hey beautiful," called a friendly voice from the back of the room. Most of the reporters were gone for the evening, and the only ones left were a group of mostly 20-ish rookie journalists who were paying their dues to move up the ranks of the *Nashville News.*

"Hiya, Charlie," smiled Carrie. Charlie was one of the few veterans who dared to watch the clock turn six in the newsroom. He and Carrie hit it off the day she walked through the doors of the *News* for the first time, and three months later, they were flirting with a relationship that both of them wanted, and both of them knew would never happen. "What are you doing here so late?"

He walked over to Carrie's desk and sat on the edge, playing with a pencil. He was an attractive man in his late twenties. His golden brown hair was cut neatly and it accented deep, coffee-brown eyes which were warm and comforting. He was wearing a pale yellow polo shirt and khaki pants; an outfit that made him look more like a college prep than a reporter. "Finishing up my story on the drug deaths in Brentwood. You have a council meeting tonight, right?"

"Yeah," Carrie sighed, falling into her chair. She leaned back and started fanning herself with her damp shirt. "I'm so sick of listening to blowhards spouting off their achievements, watching their heads grow as fast as their egos, so they can impress their fellow blowhards, who really couldn't care less."

"Waste of time."

"Usually, but maybe not tonight." Carrie looked around suspiciously and continued, speaking just above a whisper. "They are supposed to be talking about the kidnappings."

Charlie sat up straight and leaned close to Carrie. "Are you serious?"

"Yes. Can you believe it?"

"No, I can't. Does Max know?"

Max Worth was the cantankerous executive editor at the *News*. He had started working at the newspaper as a delivery boy and had put in more than 30 years doing everything from running delivery routes, to writing obituaries. He had paid his dues at the paper, and he was hell-bent on making sure that everyone that worked under him did the same. He expected to know every piece of information every reporter had. If he didn't, and he found out you held something back, you would be given the worst stories to cover … if you were allowed to keep your job.

Carrie whispered, "I haven't said a word because it isn't officially on their agenda. I heard from a source that it would likely come up. This could be my big shot, Charlie."

"It could. Or it could be Max's big shot to move you from council meetings to county fairs and quilting bees. I suggest you keep this between us, or you are going to find yourself up to your knees in pig shit."

"I'm not telling anyone if you're not."

He touched her chin gently, and headed back to his desk. "You know me," he called back.

3

The city council meeting was held in a huge granite building in the heart of downtown Nashville. Carrie always felt like a little kid when she approached the massive, three-story structure, and this night was no different.

She was wearing a black satin undershirt beneath a charcoal-grey, mid-sleeved jacket and matching slacks; it was professional, but not too dressy. She was careful to wear her soft-soled loafers to meetings, because heeled shoes made a loud announcement that you were on your way when they hit the polished stone floors.

As Carrie turned the corner of the hallway, she held her breath. Harlan Stanton was standing near the chamber doors. He was a tall man in his 60s, with a big voice and an even bigger attitude. His distaste for reporters was known throughout Nashville, and the last thing Carrie wanted was to draw his attention.

Carrie could hear Harlan's boisterous laugh, and nearly turned the other direction to escape being noticed. Glancing at her watch, she knew she was running late, and did not have time to play cat-and-mouse. She lowered her head and walked briskly toward the chamber, being careful to avoid eye contact with Harlan. It didn't work.

"Good evening, Miss Stevens," Harlan boomed down the hallway as he bowed, the buttons on his starched white shirt and gray blazer struggling to keep in his massive stomach. The men standing with him were strangers to the young reporter and simply smiled as she approached.

"Harlan, it's nice to see you," Carrie offered, giving a quick nod of acknowledgement to his acquaintances. She picked up speed to get into the room, but was halted by the councilman's massive arm reaching across the doorway.

"Now, hold up there, little lady. What's your hurry? The meeting's not going to start without its leader." He smiled a toothy smile. His face was red, and sprinkled with drops of sweat that beaded his forehead and upper lip; his full, chipmunk cheeks looked as if they would swallow his face at any moment. Harlan liked to think of himself as a true Southern gentleman, but Carrie couldn't find one aspect of the man that was gentle. A wave of onion and garlic odor smashed into Carrie's face when he spoke making the young reporter's stomach turn.

Still, Carrie mustered up a smile. "Excuse me; I have to get in there. Need to get a good seat, ya know."

"Oh, don't let me stop you. You just make sure you got your facts straight this time, little lady. Can't have any misspelling or, shall we say, misinformation in the newspaper, now can we?" His laughter echoed down the hallway as he lowered his arm to let Carrie through. She clinched her fists as she squeezed by his enormous girth and walked into the room.

The chamber was large and empty except for the actual council members and a handful of spectators. The room reminded Carrie of a courtroom with its faux wood-paneled walls, and uncomfortable wooden seats that creaked when someone dared to move while sitting on them. The council's table stretched across the front of the room, with a Tennessee state flag on one end, and the American flag on the other.

Sheriff Jimmy Tate was sitting in the front row with his cowboy boots propped on the railing separating the council table from the rest of the chamber. For a big city like Nashville, Tate always seemed to be the stereotypical "good ole' boy" sheriff you might find in a backwoods town. He was a tall, slender man in his 40s and always wore a cowboy hat and dirty boots. His face was thin and ruddy; a full, handle-bar mustache creeped its way down both sides of his mouth. A few strands of salt and pepper hair peeked out from beneath his hat. If he could have gotten away with it, Carrie was certain he'd be wearing blue jeans with his official sheriff's shirt.

Carrie slid into the second row across the center aisle from the Sheriff and took out her notebook and a small digital recorder. She needed to be out of the meeting a quickly as possible to get the story in for the next day's paper.

The room silenced with the loud bang of the chamber door closing and the thumps of Harlan's shiny, patent-leather shoes as he waddled toward the front of the room.

He made his way to the council's table and tapped on the microphone to make sure it was working. "This meeting will now come to order," he boomed.

The City Council consisted of five members, with Harlan being the ringleader of the bunch. A lifelong resident of Nashville, Harlan made his spot in the elite of the city by becoming one of the richest and most feared litigators in the Southeast. His status helped his political career, as did his immense wealth and property holdings in the county, and he won his spot on the city council 22 years ago. Rumor was that a lot of local businesses and family friends benefitted from Harlan's position with the city, and those who questioned his judgment were all but run out of town. Everyone knew Harlan, and everyone was afraid of him.

"Any new business this week?" Harlan asked, looking around the table.

Edwin Meyer, owner of Meyer's Grocery Store, one of the oldest in the county, raised his hand and was acknowledged by the council chairman. Straightening his tie, and rising, which was not required, Edwin cleared his throat and spoke boldly, "The city manager reported to me that … well … there was really nothing to report. Thank you." A small chuckle came from those in attendance, causing Edwin's face to glow red. He had been on the council for three years, and was the most ineffective member of the group. Edwin was a nervous man, and his presence on the council was the subject of a lot of rumors. People felt that his position was bought and paid for by Harlan. He could not think for himself, and usually did whatever Harlan did; he voted however Harlan voted, and he spoke when he was told to.

John Googleman and Stan Height had been on the council for five years each and they said little. John was the owner of a local chain of restaurants and the only things he worried about in council meetings were the items that were either going to harm his business or make him money. At 50 he had aspirations of running for a higher government seat, but the fact that most knew he was easily bought made a potential campaign unrealistic. Either way, he religiously attended every meeting, and spent his time at the board table chewing on jerky and reading the newspaper.

Stan, on the other hand, was rarely at council meetings. The owner of a used-car dealership, he was not seeking a re-election to the council, and couldn't care less what was being discussed. He started out strong when he first arrived on the council, but a series of questionable decisions that benefitted certain members of the council turned Stan sour on politics. When he did bother to come to meetings, it was simply to crack an off-color joke or to make smart remarks at the expense of other council members.

Billy Tyler was the newest member of the city council and Carrie's favorite. He was elected the year before in a landslide over Harlan's nephew. Having lost his wife to breast cancer, Billy was a single father of two young children, and was liked by most in the community for his strong moral stances and his push to make Nashville safe for children. Billy didn't look anywhere near his 30 years, which caused many board members, especially Harlan, to treat him like an inexperienced teenager.

"I personally would like to know what is going with these kidnappings," Billy said. His deep, blue eyes were accented by a bright, white polo shirt. His blonde hair was combed neatly except for one wayward strand that only added to his young appearance.

Harlan piped up, "Well, Billy, this is a city council meeting, not a law enforcement meeting. I suggest you attend one of Jimmy's sessions if you would like to approach this topic further."

Carrie clicked on her recorder as quietly as possible to avoid drawing Harlan's attention.

"Harlan, this is a city matter, and I think the good people of the city would like to know that their elected members at least had the decency to show a little concern." Billy's eyes flashed. He was getting worked up, but was still in control of his emotions. There was no way he was going to allow the council to brush him aside and not address a topic he felt passionately about.

"Fine," Harlan sneered at Billy. Creaking in his seat, he slowly sat back, silently letting the young councilman know that the meeting was going to be dictated by him. After a few minutes of silence, and a lot of seething, Harlan finally called the sheriff. "Jimmy would you like to come address this situation?" he asked, not taking his eyes off the young, smiling councilman.

The sheriff stood and walked slowly to the front of the room. He had a swagger that would make John Wayne green with envy. He stepped up to the microphone. "There's not much to report. We've got a lot of kids missing and very few leads."

<u>4</u>

He woke to a darkened room and the sound of crying in the corner. His mouth was dry, and as he reached up to wipe it, he then realized that it was covered with some sort of tape. The smell in the room was overwhelming; it reeked of mildew and dust, reminding him of the basement at his home after a long rain. The quiet crying in the corner was deafening.

After checking to make sure his hands and legs were not bound, he noticed a small light on the other side of the room, adjacent to the sound of whimpering, and crawled quietly to it. Focusing through a small hole in the wooden wall, he was able to see out of the room and saw nothing but trees. The sound of boots walking toward the room brought him back to reality. He scurried back to the spot where he thought he was originally and closed his eyes, pretending to be asleep and using the opportunity to pray a silent prayer.

<u>5</u>

"'m sorry, sheriff, but that's just not good enough," Billy Tyler said as the law official turned to start heading back to his seat. The sheriff paused and offered an animated sigh.

"Mr. Tyler," Harlan broke in as Sheriff Tate turned back toward the council table, "the sheriff is a very busy man, and if he doesn't ..."

"The sheriff is a servant to this community," Billy broke in, his face glowing red from anger, his voice rising, "and as a member of this community, a taxpayer, and a father, I demand to know what is being done to curb these kidnappings and catch whoever is responsible." By this time, the councilman was half-seated, half-standing, and was leaning across the table to look Harlan in the eye. He was serious about this, and there was no way any one could doubt that.

Carrie fought the urge to stand up and cheer. She looked at Harlan and noticed his face turning red as well. The room was deadly silent as everyone waited for the next move.

Harlan glared at Billy, waited for the young councilman to be seated, and then turned his attention toward the sheriff. Tate was staring at no one in particular, his mouth half open, as if someone had just slapped him across the face.

"Sheriff, is there anything else you could offer the concerned citizens about these kidnappings?" Harlan asked through gritted teeth.

The sheriff leaned in close to the mike and spoke slowly and softly, "There have been five children kidnapped from five different parks around the county. As far as we know there have been no common traits among the children, other than the fact that they were all either alone at the parks or not being watched closely by their parents or siblings. "

"Have there been any reports of suspicious people or vehicles in the area?" Billy asked.

"No. Nothing. No suspicious people, no notes, no demands, nothing."

"Have you done anything to increase security at these parks?"

Tate chuckled mockingly, glanced at Harlan, and then looked at Billy. "And what would you like me to do, councilman? There are more than 100 parks in Davidson County, and they are spread over more than 500 square miles. Would you like me to pull my deputies off other assignments, to patrol parks that *might* by hit? We might stop the kidnappings, but crime would go through the roof."

"I'm sorry, sheriff, but I refuse to believe there is absolutely nothing you can do to stop this problem. Maybe if you created some sort of task force …"

Tate leaned on the podium, his leather gun belt squeaking with the movement. "I'll tell you what, son, you fit it somewhere in that little budget of yours to get me some more officers and patrol cars, and I'll see what I can do " With that, the sheriff tipped his hat, straightened his back, and walked out of the chamber.

Once again, Billy turned his attention back to Harlan and the rest of the council. "What about forming some sort of community task force. I'm sure there are enough scared people out there who would be willing to help keep the parks safe."

"That requires money, Mr. Tyler," Harlan responded, "and as you know, we are strapped for money this year."

Carrie noticed that Billy looked defeated and deflated. Whatever answers he was looking for were not going to be revealed this night.

Harlan called for any new business, and 45 minutes later, after the normal issues of spending and complaints were addressed, the gavel fell and the room quickly emptied. Carrie wanted desperately to talk to Billy about the night's events for her story, but he disappeared quickly and quietly out the door behind the council's table. She rushed for the front door, deadline looming, when Harlan's big arm stopped her at the doorway once again.

"Quite an interesting little meeting we had," he said, smiling slightly.

"Sure was. Can't wait to get back and get it started. Now, if you'll excuse me…"

"Now, hold on, girl. Let's discuss what you are going to put in that story."

"Let's not," Carrie sneered; the nerve of that man. "If you have any concerns, after reading the paper in the morning, you feel free to call Max Worth. He'll have whatever answers you feel you deserve, Mr. Stanton. Now, if you will please move your arm, I can be on my way."

Harlan lifted his massive arm and stepped back just enough to let Carrie squeeze through the doorway once again.

She was about halfway to the exit doors when she heard him bellow down the hall, "I think I will have a little talk with your friend, Max. Yes sir, I think I will call him in the morning."

Great.

<u>6</u>

He wasn't sure what time it was, but one thing was for sure: the whimpering and stench in the room remained. It was still daylight, maybe even more daylight, as the sun sent bright rays into the little room. It was bright enough for him to make out some features, like a small twin bed in the middle of the room. The whimpering was coming from a small child lying in the corner. The boy was facing the wall, hugging his knees and rocking back and forth. He wanted to go over to the child, but feared he would startle the frightened youngster, which could cause a scream. He didn't know why he was there or who was holding him there, and he wasn't quite sure he wanted to find out just yet.

7

Carrie woke up with the alarm the next morning and struggled to lift her head off the pillow. The nights seemed shorter and shorter every day. She looked around her small apartment and sighed. It wasn't supposed to be this way.

Four years earlier, she graduated top in her class from her small Alabama high school. She had a love for writing and dreamed of working at a big city newspaper and eventually writing the best-selling book that was going to make her a household name. She wanted to be the next Patricia Cornwell or Faye Kellerman, and she knew it would be a tough road to get there.

Though she could have gotten into any state university she wanted with a full scholarship, she sent out one application to one college and prayed. Two days before graduation, she received her acceptance letter to Vanderbilt University in Nashville.

Carrie spent the entire summer working for the money she needed to buy a bus ticket to Nashville. She spent hours checking out groceries at the local store, babysitting neighbors' children, and even mowing lawns. Her family was unable to help, so she was going to have to do this on her own. Every cent she made went into a lockbox under her bed, and that August, she took her $936 and boarded the bus for her first-ever trip out of Alabama.

It would not be fitting to say that college was hard, because hard could not begin to describe those four years of her life. She was alone in a big city with no friends, so Carrie spent most nights in her dorm room studying. Her roommate, Theresa, was never home, and when she was, she was lying on her bed listening to her iPod, completely ignoring Carrie. Theresa left after the first semester, and Carrie was somehow able to secure a room to herself for the rest of her stay at Vandy.

College was nothing but studying, and sleep for Carrie. She rarely left campus, and spent whatever free time she had writing. The men that had shown any interest in her were quickly brushed away. Her sophomore year, Carrie got a part-time job at the Heard Library on campus. It was a dream job for a girl who treasured books like gold. She lived on Ramen noodles and macaroni and cheese as she squirreled away every cent she could.

Her third year brought her an internship at the *Nashville News*, and the moment she stepped in the door, she knew this was right where she needed to be. She loved the fast-paced, deadline-stressed adrenaline rush she got while shadowing reporters and the staff was pleased with her curiosity and drive.

Two days after graduating with honors from Vanderbilt, and one day after receiving her offer to become a reporter at *The News*, Carrie signed a lease on her first apartment and used most of her savings to put a down payment on a used car. Her apartment was in an area called Antioch, which was about 10 miles south of Nashville, and was known for its affordable apartments. The lease said she was renting a 2-bedroom, 1-bath apartment, but that was being generous; an oversized studio apartment was a more accurate description of the dwelling.

Her furnishings for the apartment were primitive at first. A trip to the local Salvation Army thrift store landed her a stained couch and a TV. An old card table she snagged from someone's curbside garbage and a broken folding chair held together with duct tape was her dining room. She slept on an old twin bed that the college was getting rid of, and milk crates from the local dairy covered in sheets served as her dresser.

It wasn't a lot, but it was all hers.

Carrie had just stepped out of the shower when the phone began to ring. Of course. She ran dripping into the living room and was greeted with an angry-sounding Max. "I need you to get here, now." He slammed down the phone before she could ask what was wrong, and Carrie could feel fear beginning to well up. She couldn't imagine what she could have done wrong.

It took her 15 minutes to dry off, throw on a simple, pastel green cotton peasant shirt, khaki pants and a pair of brown loafers, dry her hair, and put on a hint of make-up. Surprisingly, the traffic was not bad, so she was walking into the newsroom exactly 40 minutes after receiving Max's call. She was just about to knock on his office door when it flew open and she was suddenly face to face with the editor. "Have a seat and I'll be right back."

She walked into the large room and sat on a faux-leather chair in front of his massive oak desk. The walls were painted white and were covered with framed articles and pictures of Max with famous country music singers. Large frames held Max's degree from the University of Tennessee and an award from 1995. Like Max, his desk was big and cluttered. A computer sat on another desk against the back wall. At the front of the office were a round table and two chairs. The table was covered with older issues of the *News* and copies of *The New York Times, The Washington Post,* and *The Dallas Morning News.*

Carrie sat and worried for about 10 minutes before Max walked back into the room and closed the door. She knew something was wrong the minute the door clicked shut. Max was known to keep his door open at all times, even when situations warranted it shut. There was a story about a reporter being fired years ago, and the newsroom drawing silent as everyone listened to the conversation. The man's sobs could be heard across the newsroom.

Max was a short, stocky man, no taller than about 5'10". His thin, graying hair had not seen a comb in years, and his white shirt was usually stained with the morning's breakfast drippings. He always wore khaki pants and black dress shoes that had never been shined. Stress and frustration had left their mark on his face, and worked their way through the pock marks that covered his cheeks and neck. His eyes were dark, nearly black, and could cut to the soul of anyone that dared to anger the former baseball star.

He walked around the desk and sat in a leather office chair. "So, I hear the meeting was interesting last night."

"Yes, sir. Nothing major, of course, but they did talk about the kidnappings a bit."

"I saw that. I also saw a lack of interviews."

Carrie swallowed hard. "Yes, sir. I tried to catch Billy, but he rushed out. No one else said much."

"I also received a phone call from Harlan Stanton this morning. He said you refused to talk to him and that he would have been more than happy to give you an interview."

Harlan was happy to speak with anyone if it meant publicity. Also, it gave him fodder for his complaints about the media. "Yes, sir. I just felt that Harlan wasn't going to say much more than what he thought would benefit him. He didn't offer much at the meeting, and didn't think he would offer much to my story, either."

A smile slowly worked its way across Max's face. "That was a good, sound journalistic decision."

"Thank you."

"Still, an interview is an interview." Max leaned back in his chair and rubbed his face with both hands. Whatever he was going to say next was obviously troubling him. "You know, Carrie, I've seen you grow these past few months. You came here a rookie reporter, you watched, you learned, and it shows." Max turned around in his seat and opened the bottom drawer of the computer desk. He retrieved two plastic, clear Solo cups and a bottle of Jack Daniels. He placed the cups on the desk in front of Carrie, opened the whiskey bottle and poured a little more than a shot's worth in each cup. "Here, have a drink."

"No thank you, sir. I'm really not a drinker."

He drank the shot and slammed the cup down on the desk. "Carrie, I'm letting you go."

She grabbed the cup in front of her and drank the liquor, wincing as the alcohol quickly burned the back of her throat. "You're, what?"

"I'm letting you go." Carrie could feel his eyes piercing hers, waiting in anticipation for this small, weak woman in front of him to curl up in a ball and start sobbing uncontrollably. Truth was that was what she felt like doing. Instead she straightened her back and set the cup down on his desk hard. She was too stunned, too angry to give him the satisfaction of crying. "Well," she finally said, her voice cracking under the strain of the news and the aftermath of the whiskey, "I guess I'll just get my things packed and be on my way." She stood and started walking toward the door, fighting the lump in her throat.

"I was hoping you would react this way. I knew I made a wise decision."

Carrie spun on her heels, stomped up to Max's desk and slammed her hands down. The tears came, finally, but they were not streaming from sadness, but burning down her cheeks from rage. "You made the right decision? You made the right decision!" She was ranting like a child and knew it, but the words seemed caught in the emotion that was still stuck in her throat.

"Carrie, sit down."

"Why, Max? So you can tell me what a fine young lady I am and then suggest I make my living selling my body out on Murfreesboro Road? Hey, I know, tell me how intelligent I am and then suggest I start flipping burgers at McDonald's." Her voice was growing louder, but she did not notice that every eye in the newsroom was firmly planted on her. "Because that's where I'm going to be, Max. Offering fries to fat people at McDonald's. No one in this industry is going to hire a reporter who was fired less than a year after starting." The tears were flowing like a river. She was defeated.

"Are you through?" Max asked softly, handing Carrie a tissue.

She took the tissue and shook her head yes, unable to find any more words.

"You are not going to have a problem finding a job. In fact, I have one lined up for you."

Carrie looked up from behind the now-soaked napkin. "What?"

"Let me introduce you to your new boss."

He waved toward the office window behind Carrie, the door opened, and Harlan Stanton walked into the room.

<u>8</u>

He became accustomed to the routine rather quickly. A person –
a man in a dark mask – came in every morning with a plate of
food for each of the boys. The crying boy in the corner was
named Thomas, and he had been in this room for a long time. There
really was no way to tell what day it was until the sun set or rose,
shining its light through the gaps in the walls.

Once the food was delivered, the boys would take the tape off their
mouths and inhale whatever was left for them. This happened twice a
day, once after the sun rose, and once just before the sun set. The food
was good, he had to admit. He knew the man killed his own food,
because he often heard gunshots in the distance and then would hear
the man working outside, probably skinning the kill.

He was the one who did all the talking, and it was always in a
whisper. He, at first, was irritated because there was never a response
to his questions, but he was thrilled to have company in the small
room. It was a sense of security, even though they were not certain
either of them would survive this ordeal in the end.

That morning, the food was delivered as usual. "My name is
Stephen." He wasn't sure why he spoke. Maybe it was to reassure
himself that he was really still alive; that this wasn't all just a
nightmare.

"Thank you," Thomas answered in a shaky voice and went back to
eating.

"I'm getting out of here," Stephen said without looking up.

"How?"

"He will bring us food as usual. His guard is down because he isn't
afraid of us. He knows we are too afraid to do anything, plus, we are
just a couple of kids. When he opens that door, I'm going to tackle
him, knock him down, and run out into the woods. I'll have the
darkness to help me."

Thomas said nothing, but Stephen knew he was listening.

"You can come with me if you want."

9

"Have you lost your mind?" was on the tip of Carrie's tongue, but the words would not work their way past her lips. She staggered backwards in the office, and fell into the chair, limp, like a worn-out doll tossed aside by a child. She couldn't hear what was being said around her, and probably didn't want to, either.

The rest of the meeting played like a bad detective novel. Harlan was genuinely upset over the recent kidnappings, and he was frustrated with the lack of progress being made by the Sheriff's Office. He wanted the case solved, but more importantly, he wanted some publicity – a white horse he could ride all the way to the governor's mansion. He saw his chance when a rumor landed in the form of a memo days earlier: *The News* was struggling to survive financially. Cue the light bulb over his head.

A quick call to Max, and some negotiations that morning had landed Harlan what he wanted. He would hire Carrie, and, along with a private detective, use her as his personal investigative reporter. Together they would dig into the kidnapping case, find the perpetrator, Carrie would write the story, sell it to *The News*, and Harlan would get props for bringing it all together. It was a win-win-win situation for all involved.

Carrie was speechless. Everything about this plan seemed unethical. So, she said the first thing that popped into her mind. "Thanks, but no thanks." With that, she stood up and headed for the door.

Max rose and quickly blocked the door before she reached it. She tried to barrel through, but it was like hitting a brick wall. "Just wait, Carrie. Let's talk this through."

"No, Max. I think I've heard enough. Even if the cause is noble, the thought of working with this … this … piece of human waste … no. I can't do it."

"Now wait one goddamn minute," Harlan raged, nearly breaking the snug-fitting chair as he stood quickly, crimson streaks climbing his neck and pooling in his cheeks. "I don't need this. I WON'T HEAR THIS from some low-life, speck of flea shit."

"Low life?" Carrie whirled around and stepped within inches of the big man's face. "You are calling me a low life?"

"Yes, Missy, I am."

Carrie struggled as hard to keep her clinched fists by her side as Harlan did to keep his conniving smirk hidden.

Max smartly stepped in between the two. "Now, we are going to talk this through, like it or not. You both need to sit down and listen."

Reluctantly the rookie reporter and councilman sat in chairs as far away from each other as the cramped space would allow.

Max walked back behind his desk and sat slowly and deliberately in his chair, placing his elbows on the desk and intertwining his fingers. "Harlan, you approached me with this offer. If you want to walk away from it, that is your prerogative. Carrie, if I were you, I would think long and hard before walking away from this."

Carrie knew he was right. If she wanted to continue her career as a journalist and still be able to remain in Nashville, this was her only option. There weren't a lot of reporting jobs out there, especially for novice journalists looking for work in a big city; but, the thought of working with Harlan seemed impossible.

After what seemed like hours of silence, Max sat back in his seat, folded his arms over his chest and looked at Harlan. "Alright, then. What next?"

The red was slowly starting to drain from Harlan's cheeks. He leaned forward, straightened his necktie, and glanced at Carrie before answering. "Tonight, Miss Stevens will meet with me and her partner on this case. The stipulations of this little job will be worked out and we will be on our way."

"Does that sound ok with you, Carrie?" Max asked.

"How much will I be paid?" Carrie asked in a whisper. She could feel a shiver of agitation welling in her chest, working its way through her body. She struggled to maintain her composure.

"You want to know that," Harlan smirked, "and you will show up tonight. Eight o'clock at Prime on Broadway." With that, the councilman stood, straightened his tie yet again, buttoned his jacket, and strolled dramatically out of the room.

Carrie was unable to stop the tears from falling. "How could you, Max," she managed to choke out, not bothering to hide her pain anymore. She wanted him to know she was crushed.

Max came around the desk and sat on top of it in front of her. He leaned forward and spoke as gently as she had ever heard him speak. "Carrie, we didn't have a choice. We have been in the red for months, and were throwing around the possibility of either closing or merging with another company. Either way, you would have been out of a job. When Harlan came in, he made an offer we could not pass up."

"At my expense."

"Maybe, but at least you are keeping a job." Max leaned back and sighed. "Look, I know this isn't ideal for you, and I know the thought of working with Harlan is … well … sickening, but you can do this. You have an opportunity in front of you that you would be a fool to pass up. The chance to help solve a case … to help save lives? Journalists dream of this kind of story. Here you are, a rookie reporter … make your mark, Carrie. Run with this."

Carrie stood up, defeated, but catching a glimmer of light at the end of the tunnel. Max was right; she would be a fool to pass up this opportunity. She needed time to think. She stuck out her hand to Max. "It's been a pleasure, Max."

Max shook her hand and opened the door to the office. "Good luck," he said, patting her on the back as she walked out of the room. She could feel all eyes in the newsroom, including Charlie's on her. She glanced at her concerned friend and gave him a smile. If she had known it would be the last time she saw him, she would have done more.

<u>10</u>

Carrie spent the afternoon doing some soul searching. She drove to her thinking spot, a lake on the outskirts of town, and sat under a large elm tree. Charlie had brought her here one day when they had flirted with the possibility of dating. It was that day that Carrie chose this to be her spot. The one place she could come and clear her mind.

She closed her eyes and listened to the leaves dancing in the air as they made their fateful fall to the ground. She heard the water lap gently against the shore and the birds serenading each other with music that would have made Mozart proud. Not once, since she started coming to this place, had Carrie ever been interrupted by the presence of another human. That day was no different.

She spent an hour mulling over this important decision, and in the end, she knew what she had to do.

Carrie arrived at the restaurant that night as promised. Prime on Broadway was the most expensive steak house in the area and was located in the heart of downtown. It was known to be a favorite spot for the rich and famous to dine. In fact, it offered mandatory valet parking, and there was always a reporter from some gossip magazine or television show loitering around the front.

Carrie had never been in the restaurant, but knew its reputation, so she chose to wear a backless, black dinner dress. Her hair was pulled in a tight bun, and she was wearing a little too much makeup. Harlan was waiting in front of the restaurant hoping to see a celebrity and get his picture taken.

"My don't you look pretty," he said with a smile, his eyes shifting around, making sure everyone in the immediate area knew this beautiful woman who was young enough to be his daughter, was with him. He was dressed in a grey, pin-striped, three-piece suit, and wore enough cologne to make Carrie's eyes water.

"Thank you," she mumbled, wanting desperately to get inside the building and out of the spotlight.

The inside of the restaurant was dark and aromatic. The host was wearing a black tuxedo and a snobbish attitude. He smiled and greeted Harlan by name and gave a condescending glance at Carrie. Harlan walked like he owned the place, speaking loudly and recognizing people from across the room. The host quickly led them to the back of the dining room. The table and chairs were covered in white linen. The dishes were China, and sparkled amid the glow of the tapers burning in the center of the table. Carrie had never been in an establishment so elegant, and she suddenly felt like poor white trash.

They were both staring at the overpriced menu items when they were interrupted by someone clearing his throat. Carrie looked at the source of the interruption.

"Good evening," said the man, gently but with authority. He was young, not much older than Carrie, with Emerald green eyes, and long, shaggy hair that was haphazardly pulled into a loose ponytail. Instead of the suit and ties that everyone in the restaurant wore, he looked comfortable in a too-large, blue, button-up shirt and faded blue jeans. The unkempt stubble on his chin brought out the chiseled features of his face.

Harlan looked up with irritated eyes and nodded his head in the direction of the empty chair next to Carrie. "Miss Stevens, I would like to introduce you to your partner in this little endeavor. Robert Holten, this is Miss Carrie Stevens."

Robert reached out and softly shook Carrie's hand, "You can call me Rob." He smiled a smile that made Carrie's heart skip a beat. She could not remember ever meeting a man so attractive.

"Pleasure to meet you," she nearly stuttered.

"Let's order," Harlan said, "and then we can get down to business."

They all ordered over-priced steak dinners with various types of potatoes and salads and sipped wine while waiting for their first course to arrive. Carrie couldn't help but feel out of place in the eatery and she realized it was really the first time she had ever been offered a meal with wine. She found herself worrying about the details of the dinner like where to place her napkin and which fork was used with which course. It was intense enough that little beads of sweat began popping up on her forehead.

To her surprise, the meal went without a hitch, and the trio dined in silence. Carrie noticed Rob glance at her a few times, and when their eyes finally did meet, he offered a warm smile.

After Harlan finished his last bite of steak, he pushed his plate to the side and took two thick envelopes from his jacket pocket and laid them on the table.

Here we go, thought Carrie, not quite sure what to expect. Rob acted as if he hadn't noticed Harlan and continued eating his steak without a word.

"Ok, let's get down to business," Harlan finally said. Rob put down his fork, crossed his arms on the table, and cocked his head in an outward show of either extreme interest or extreme defiance. If Harlan noticed, he did not say so.

"Robert, you are going to find out who is taking these little children around here. I have sources in the Sheriff's Office who will be more than willing to offer you any assistance they can in your search. Carrie, you are going to help Robert in any way you can and document the search. You will have full access to the newsroom and archive at *The News*. Once the person is caught, you will sell your story to *The News*, get your old job back, and I'll move into the governor's mansion. Any questions?" He ended the speech with his infamous toothy smile, and sat back in his chair, pleased with himself. Carrie was confused by Harlan's cut-and-dry take on the matter. Was it really going to be that simple, she wondered?

Rob leaned forward and gave Harlan a stern look. It was a silent battle of the egos, and Carrie was enjoying the show. "Yeah, I have a few questions. First of all, I assume these envelopes here contain some sort of monetary compensation?"

Harlan nodded, obviously irritated by Rob's question and attitude. Carrie sensed a slight air of discomfort emanating from the big man, but if he was threatened in any way by Rob's attitude, he was not showing it.

Silence.

"Ok, so, why don't we cut the dramatics, and you tell me what you are paying us for this job."

Harlan smirked at Rob and sat forward, leaning across the table. He looked around to make sure no one was listening, and said, in a low voice, "I am paying you $50,000. I think that is suitable for what should be a short-term job," he turned his eyes to Carrie. "I am paying you the equivalent of a year's salary at the newspaper -- $32,000." He smiled arrogantly and turned his sights back on Rob. "Satisfied?"

Rob frowned and glanced at Carrie. "Actually, Harlan, no I am not. She should be paid just as much as I am, because she will be doing just as much work. Also, we will both need reliable transportation. This is a big county, Harlan, and we will likely be driving from one end of the county to the other each day, and I don't want either of us getting stuck out in the sticks. Those are my terms. What about you," he looked at Carrie and smiled. She shook her head and looked at the councilman.

Even in the dimly-lit restaurant, Carrie could see Harlan's face turning a dark shade of crimson. "Anything else?" Harlan growled through gritted teeth. He seemed to struggle to stay in his chair.

"Not at the moment, Harlan," Rob said smugly, "but if I think of something else, I'll be sure and let you know."

Harlan shifted in his seat again as the furniture groaned under the pressure of his girth. "Fine. Now, here are some of my stipulations. One, you will report to me once a week on your progress, and none of this e-mailing. You both will meet me in my office on Friday afternoons at 4 p.m. Secondly, you will mention my name to no one during your investigation. If I am tied to this in any manner, the deal is off. You will both be out of jobs and I can personally guarantee that neither of you will find work in this town again. Do I make myself clear?"

Carrie and Rob both nodded. Harlan continued, "Half of your pay is in these envelopes. The rest will be paid at the end of this little journey. Carrie, I will give you the extra money when we all meet up again tomorrow at 4 p.m. in my office. I will hand you the keys to your transportation at that time."

Harlan stood up and dropped two $100 bills on the table. "I am running this show, Mr. Holton. It would be wise to remember that."

11

When Carrie arrived home, she sat down on her worn, used couch and opened the envelope. Everything in her heart told her that what she was doing was wrong in some way, but the money ... it was more money than she had ever seen in her life. Lord knew she needed it.

She fingered the crisp bills for an hour, even smelled them a time or two. She looked around the cramped apartment and started spending the money in her mind. She could move into a new place, buy some real furniture, get a wardrobe that didn't come from Goodwill or Wal-Mart. She could really make all the years of scrimping and saving and hard work pay off.

It was a dream come true, but why did she feel so guilty? Her thoughts were interrupted by the phone ringing.

"Hi, Carrie, It's Rob."

She jumped up and half ran into the bedroom. She stopped in front of the mirror and began straightening her hair and checking her makeup. How did he get her number? Did it really matter at that point? "Hi, Rob," she said in a squeaky voice that sounded more like a teenager's than her own.

"I thought we could meet up tomorrow before we went to Harlan's office. Maybe get a game plan together. What do you think?" Did he just chuckle, she wondered.

She wanted to scream, "Of course!" Calm, cool, collected, she said to herself. She plopped down on the bed. "Sounds great."

"Good. There's a little restaurant on the east side of downtown, just off Broadway, called Donna's Diner. Want to meet there for lunch, say, 12:30?"

"Sounds great. See you then."

She hung up the phone and stared at the ceiling. She felt like a school girl who had just been asked to the prom by the star football player. "It's just business," she told herself, a smile spread across her face.

Donna's Diner was a hole in the wall restaurant at the end of a run-down strip mall near the Cumberland River. Every store in the building had closed, every window covered with graffiti.

Carrie parked her car in front of the diner's grime encrusted doors and walked quickly inside the building. The wear and tear of age had taken its toll on the small eatery. Booths with cracked vinyl seats lined the walls, and mismatched tables and chairs filled the rest of the dining room. The floor, which had once been white, had turned brown with age, and the walls were covered in a film that hid their once-beige softness. The air was filled with the aroma of old cooking oil and grease. A broken jukebox sat in the corner.

Rob was sitting in the back of the restaurant, one of only three people in the room. Carrie climbed in the booth and said hi. He smiled and handed her a menu. Years of dirty hands and the thick blanket of grease that seemed to hang in the air made the menu nearly unreadable.

"Glad you found the place OK," he said before looking back down. He was wearing a white t-shirt and was clean shaven. As much as she hated to admit it, to him, this was all business. She, on the other hand, had spent an hour deciding what to wear, and had finally decided on a simple olive-green button-up shirt and Capri's.

They sat in silence for a few minutes before the waitress arrived. Both ordered cheeseburgers and fries.

"So," Carrie began to end the uncomfortable silence, "what is the plan?"

"Well, I've been looking at the police reports, and I think we should start with the first missing kid." He laid the file he had been staring at on the table and pushed it toward Carrie. "The kid's name is E.J. Kilmer. He's 6 years old and went missing from the Fullerton section of town. Do you know where that is?"

"I've heard of it," Carrie said, opening the folder. A small, dark face stared at her from a school picture. "I've never been there, though."

"That's probably for the best. It's on the east side of town; high drug area, but one of the cleaner neighborhoods. The people there have lived there since before the gangs moved in. They fought hard to keep their neighborhood crime-free, and for the most part, they have succeeded."

"So, when do you want to head there? I think we should start as soon as possible."

They were interrupted by the waitress bringing their food. The burgers were small and greasy, but had good flavor.

Rob took a large bite, chewed slowly, swallowed and wiped his mouth. "I think we should finish up here, head to Harlan's, and then go to Fullerton after that."

"Sounds good to me."

They made eye contact for a couple of seconds, and Carrie thought she saw a hint of a smile start to cross Rob's lips before he looked down at his plate and took another bite.

12

S tephen spent the next few days learning the routine. He wanted to know every move the masked man made every day. It was easy to remember. The man opened the door, took exactly three steps into the room, laid the plates down, turned and walked out of the room, shutting and locking the door behind him.

The plan was simple; when the man turned to leave the room, Thomas would run as fast as he could, knock the man down, and run out of the house. The problem was that he needed Thomas' help, and that was going to be difficult to get.

13

Harlan's office sat on the third floor of the AT&T building, one of the newest high rises in downtown Nashville that was affectionately called the "Batman Building" by the locals. Nashville is a big city with a small-town, Southern charm that residents take pride in. To have a modern building of this magnitude jut high in the sky and overlook the old buildings that had stood the test of time was a sign of pride for most.

The building was the tallest in Tennessee, and got its nickname from the two antennas that reached into the sky and made it look like Batman's mask. To have an office there was a sign of prestige.

Carrie and Rob rode the elevator to the 23rd floor and found his office at the end of the hallway. Once inside they were ordered by a secretary to sit and wait for Harlan who was, of course, in an important meeting. The waiting room, like the secretary, was stuffy, and obviously not used much. Carrie got the impression that it was there only to give an air of importance. Three faux-leather chairs sat around a small, oak coffee table that held strategically-placed, high-society magazines like *The New Yorker*. Fake plants sat in the corner, and music played softly from a small speaker in the ceiling. Carrie noticed that there was not a speck of dust in the entire place.

Rob was obviously uncomfortable, and began to grumble about the lack of *Sports Illustrated* magazines in the room. He finally sat down across the room from Carrie and pulled out his cell phone.

They sat there for what seemed like an hour before they were finally informed that Mr. Stanton would see them now. Rob made a goofy face and rolled his eyes, causing Carrie to snicker. They walked down a small hall and entered a large office at the end.

The room was covered in fake wood panels, and was much bigger than any office needed to be. Harlan sat behind a large cedar desk that held a computer monitor, keyboard, and a desk calendar. That was it. No papers, in-boxes, files, or anything else that indicated that actual work occurred there on a daily basis. Carrie wondered how much the space was needed for actual work, and how much the space was needed to hold Harlan's ego.

The pair was ordered to sit in two chairs in front of the desk by Harlan's finger. The councilman was on the phone, and he made it clear that the call was much more important than they were. Carrie found herself getting increasingly annoyed by Harlan's boisterous laugh and showboating. She even wondered if the councilman was really talking to anyone at all.

Fifteen minutes later, Harlan hung up the phone and leaned across the desk.

"Well, good afternoon Miss Stevens … Rob. What do you say we get right down to business?" The big man opened a drawer and pulled out two packages of papers and two envelopes. He laid them on the desk and began explaining.

They were formal contracts laying out the agreement made in the restaurant the night before. In addition, the pair was to go to Nashville Ford and pick up their rental automobiles – two Ford Focuses. The contract called for the pair to use the cars only for official business, etc. Harlan found it necessary to treat the duo as if they were three years old and read the entire contract to them word-for-word.

After he finished, he pushed the papers across the table for Carrie and Rob to look over and sign. Both did quickly. They were then handed their rental agreements, shook hands with Harlan, and headed out the door.

"Well, that was fun. All that waiting was longer than the actual meeting," Rob laughed once they were outside the building. He put on his sunglasses and looked up at the massive structure. It was so tall that no one could see the top when standing outside the front doors. "I can't believe he has an office in there. It must cost him thousands in rent; and for what … to show off?"

"Well, when you have an ego like that, and you're looking to make your move to the capital, I guess you have to at least make yourself look important," Carrie said.

14

C arrie and Rob picked up their cars at the dealership and parked Rob's in a public lot on the east side of downtown before heading to their first destination.

The Fullerton neighborhood was small, old, and decaying. The sounds of children playing echoed, though they were not visible from the main street. The shadows of the large oak trees that filled the small yards danced on the streets, making the place seem lively; but, there was something in the air that brought feelings of sorrow. This was the area that started it all. The first missing child, E.J. Kilmer had disappeared from a local park several weeks ago, and fear still lingered in the air.

Carrie and Rob had decided that this was the perfect place to start their investigation. They pulled onto Fuller Street and stopped the car in front of the park where the road dead-ended.

"This must be the place," Carrie noted, sadly. Despite the bad reputation the area seemed to have, the park was well taken care of with freshly-mowed grass.

Rob looked up from the police report he had been reading since they got in the car. "Yep, this is it. Fuller Park. Report says that E.J. had come to the park with his brother, Tyrone, and was watching his brother and some other boys playing basketball. Tyrone said that one minute little E.J. was sitting next to the court, and the next minute he was gone."

"So sad. Was there anyone suspicious in the area?"

Rob shook his head. "Nope; no one noticed anything, though that may just be the way people roll around here."

"What do you mean?"

Rob closed the file folder holding the report and looked at the naïve reporter. "This is not a great area, Carrie. The people here do not trust the police, and I don't blame them. These kids have grown up with their parents telling them horror stories about their run-ins with the police. I wouldn't talk either, if I were them. I think we should talk to the parents in the area. If the kids did talk, they are more likely to have talked to their parents."

Rob began walking down Fuller Street going door to door and Carrie began trudging across the park toward a group of teenage boys standing near the basketball court. As she walked, she tried to picture the day E.J. disappeared. Was it sunny? Warm? She envisioned the children playing without a care in the world. Then, in an instant, terror strikes. Panic hits the brother. Where was E.J.? How did it feel to go home and admit to his mother that he could not find his brother? The boy must be ravaged with guilt, she thought.

Carrie reached the group, all of whom had turned to stare at her. "Hi, fellas," she nearly stuttered. "My name is Carrie, and I am looking for some information on the missing boy from around here. Anyone want to talk to me?"

"You da police?" one of the teens asked. He looked to be about 15 or 16 and was obviously the ringleader of the group. He was shirtless, revealing numerous scars on his ebony skin, some of which appeared to be fairly new. His dark boxer shorts sat just above a pair of too-big jeans that were sitting just below his butt. The sneer on his face made Carrie feel like running, but she stood her ground.

"No, I'm not. I'm actually a reporter."

"So, you can make us famous?" The teen moved closer, a wicked smirk crossing his face.

Carrie began backing up, and slipped her hand in the pocket of her jeans. Attached to her key chain was a small can of pepper spray.

The group was moving closer, about to corner her against the fence, when a voice rose from behind the boys. "Leave her alone."

The boys turned and separated just enough that Carrie could see the source of the sound. A tall teen, about 17 years old, was standing with his hands on his hips. "Leave her alone," he repeated in an even tone of voice.

"We just messin' around Ty," the ringleader said, stepping back from Carrie. "We wasn't gonna hurt her."

"Whatever, Rodney. Lady, you best be comin' with me." He stretched out a long, dark arm and hand, which Carrie grasped.

She squeezed her way through the group and stood next to Ty. Slowly, the group of teens began to disperse, mumbling under their breath as they walked away. She turned to Ty. "Thank you."

Without saying a word, the young man nodded, turned and began walking away. Carrie stared as he walked, and then it hit her. "Ty. Tyrone. You're E.J.'s brother, aren't you?"

The teen seemed to flinch at the sound of his brother's name being called. He paused mid-stride and seemed frozen in time for what seemed like minutes. Finally his shoulder rose and fell as he took a long, deep breath, turned and faced Carrie. "Yes, I am."

"I'd like to talk to you."

"I already talked to the police."

"That's all well, but I would like to talk to you. I'm not the police."

Ty pondered her request and finally said "OK." They walked to a nearby bench and sat down.

It didn't take long for the young man to start telling his story.

Ty was 16 years old. When he was 10 and his brother was a baby, not even a year old, their mother dropped them off at their aunt's house. She never came back. Ty was sure she was either in jail or dead. His aunt, Dolores, tried to take care of the two boys, but she was not mother material and was battling her own demons. She would often disappear for days, leaving Ty to take care of his brother.

At the age of 13, Ty quit school and got a job at a local grocery store stocking shelves. The money he made went to buy food and other necessities. He was determined to make sure his brother got an education and wasn't burdened with survival like he had been.

When Ty was 15, his aunt was arrested and put in jail on drug charges. He and E.J. had been on their own ever since. Ty was working two jobs and taking on the responsibility of being father and brother. Many a day had he spent rooting through the dumpster behind the store in search for dented cans of vegetables and stale loaves of bread. Several of the workers in the store knew Ty's story and would buy him lunch meat and other items to help him out.

The day the boy disappeared, Ty was enjoying his first day off in months. They had gone to the park to play basketball. E.J. was sitting on the dirt next to the court playing with his cars. He was only feet away from the basketball court. Then, it seemed like he vanished into thin air. The teens all spread out and searched the neighborhood for E.J., but he was nowhere to be found. His cars were still lying on the ground.

Ty didn't know what to do. If he went to the police, they would take them away; but, how would he ever find his brother? A neighbor finally called the police, and all of Ty's fears were extinguished when the officers arrived and did a half-assed investigation. Seems the disappearance of a little black boy from a not-so-nice neighborhood was not one of their top priorities. They spoke with a couple of the teens, got a statement from Ty, and were never seen again.

Telling the story was taking its toll on the teen. Tears were rolling down his face and Carrie found herself crying, too. Once he finished his tale, he rose and walked away, leaving Carrie sitting there with a thousand unanswered questions rolling around in her head.

15

E.J. heard the footsteps coming closer to the door and covered his head. The dark room was scary, but he learned quickly to fight his demons of fear and sit quietly until the big man in the mask left his plate of food and left.

He knew there were other kids in the house, because he could hear them talking. He could tell they were both boys. He desperately wanted to sneak into their room for company, but he was afraid of the boogeyman.

16

Carrie and Rob met at the car. His search had been futile. No one was willing to talk to him, at least those who bothered to answer the door. Carrie shared her conversation with Ty and how she felt about what happened.

"I questioned us doing this," she admitted to Rob, "until I talked to him. Now I see we have to do this. No one seems to care."

"Well, I think we have exhausted all we can here. Let's head to the spot the next kid was taken and see what we can come up with there. I handed out cards with our numbers on it. Hopefully, someone will call."

They travelled across town to the scene of the second abduction. Wendell Thomas Freeson was at the park with his grandmother. They went to the park nearly every afternoon after the 10 year old got home from school. The grandmother, Olivia Riley, always sat on a park bench under a large oak tree adjacent to the playground. She was reading a book that afternoon, as she did each day. Wendell was playing football with a group of friends.

Olivia admittedly lost track of time, and when she noticed it was going on 5:00, she got up and walked to the field where the boys were playing. Wendell was not there. The other boys said that they thought Wendell had gone home.

Another child had seemingly vanished into thin air.

Carrie and Rob pulled up to the park and left the car sitting on the side of Grey Street. The park was quiet. There were few people there, but as Carrie looked down at her watch, she noticed it was nearly 7:00; a little late for children to be frolicking at the playground.

"Olivia's house is over there," Rob said pointing to a small, yellow wooden house across the street from the park. An older Mercury sedan was sitting in the driveway and a lamp in the window was on. "Let's see if she would be willing to talk to us."

The pair walked across the quiet street. A white-washed fence surrounded the property, but the gate was open, so there was no worry about a dog jumping out at them. From the looks of the yard, the woman was conscious about neatness. The walkway was lined with impatiens and there was not a weed in sight. The front porch was empty except for a swing dangling in front of the window. Rob opened the screen door and knocked on the front door. Within seconds they heard slippers shuffling across a hardwood floor.

"Who is it," came an older voice from inside.

"Mrs. Riley?" Carrie asked softly.

"Yes. Who's calling?"

"My name is Carrie Stevens and I am an investigative reporter. We are looking into the disappearance of Wendall and would really like to talk to you."

After several seconds of silence, the click of the deadbolt, and the turn of the door lock broke the uncertainty and the door, opened slightly. Carrie noticed it was still chained to the wall.

"I've already spoken to the police about this. Why don't you talk to them?"

"Well, Mrs. Riley, I like to get my information from a person, not a piece of paper. I would really like to hear what you can offer me on this. I know it is hard, but I want to help find your grandson."

The soft, baby blue eyes peering from behind the door seemed trusting, yet vulnerable. The door closed, and the chain was removed. It then reopened, revealing a woman who looked much older than her 53 years. She was small, barely over five feet tall, and frail. Years of laughter and tears had left their mark on her face and hands.

The house was smaller than it appeared from the outside. A worn couch, two recliners, and a console TV took up most of the space in the living room. The carpet was burnt-orange shag that was popular in the 70s, but not since. The walls were covered with antique, flowered wallpaper that had begun peeling near the ceiling. The top of the TV was covered with framed photos that were covered with a dust that made the air difficult to breathe.

Carrie and Rob sat on the couch, sending another poof of dust in the air. They declined the older woman's offer of drinks and cookies.

"Obviously, this is difficult for me," Olivia began, pulling a tissue from a box on the coffee table in anticipation of the tears that were likely going to fall. "My daughter, Wendell's mother, has not spoken to me since that day. I know she blames me."

"Can you tell us what happened," Rob asked.

Olivia looked at him like it was the first time she noticed he was in the room. "I don't know. He was playing with his friends like he always did. I can still hear them laughing and yelling. Then, he was gone."

"Did you watch him every afternoon?" Carrie asked.

"Yes," the woman shifted in her chair. "Actually, he lived with me … for about three years now."

"May I ask why?"

"Julia, my daughter, had Wendell when she was very young, and she's just not right," the woman tapped her head, "up here. She couldn't take care of herself, much less a baby. So, one night, she came by crying; asked if Wendell could stay with me. What could I say?"

"Was Wendell like his mother … in the head?" Rob asked.

"Lord, no. No, he is smart. If you talked to him, you never would know he was only 10. He talks like an adult. Thinks like an adult, too."

"So, tell me about the day Wendell disappeared," Carrie inquired softly.

Olivia shifted in her chair again, and looked down at the tissue in her hands. She began tearing it into pieces. "I was sitting in the park, just reading, like I did every day. I didn't worry about him at that park. His friends were always there. They always played together, looked out for each other, so it was real relaxing for me. That day, I lost track of the time. When I looked at my watch and noticed it was dinner time, I got up, closed my book, and made my way over to where they were playing. Only, he wasn't there."

She dabbed her eyes with the shredded tissue and continued. "Funny thing was I really wasn't worried. We lived right across the street. I just figured he had gone to the bathroom or something. So I just stood there. The kids had said that they thought he had gone home. I waited there, and then I realized he was gone. I walked across the street to the house, back to the park. He was gone." Olivia broke down into sobs, buried her head in her hands, and tried to catch her breath.

Carrie could feel emotion gathering in her throat and she fought the urge to join Mrs. Riley. She felt her pain. She could picture the panic the grandmother must have gone through when she realized her grandson was not at the park. She could imagine the woman's chest tightening in fear, her breath becoming difficult to take; her mind trying to focus on breathing while flooded with the worry of Wendell. She must have felt like she was drowning in fear.

Carrie rose from the couch and put her arm around Olivia's shaking shoulders. She leaned close to the woman's ear and whispered, "We are going to find him, Mrs. Riley, I promise. We will find Wendell and bring him back to you."

Olivia raised her head and looked at Carrie with pleading eyes, "Thank you. Please bring my Thomas home."

17

Finding the children was easy for him, but it was not a quick process. It took days of scoping out the parks and observing their mannerisms before he could even begin to focus on the next victim. He only needed one more to complete his mission.

He was sitting on a bench next to the basketball court, watching the children play in a playground about 100 feet in front of him. It was a hot day, much too hot for his long-sleeved shirt, jeans, work boots and gloves. He was surprised that no one ever seemed to notice how out of place he was.

His victim was playing on the jungle gym. He came to the park every day after school with his big sister who seemed more interested in making out with her boyfriend than she did in keeping an eye on her brother. He was always alone. The other children seemed to pick on him as much as they ignored him. He had to be about six or seven years old. Perfect.

Today was the day they would meet. It would be a simple eye-to-eye contact; nothing big. The next day they would talk. He knew the boy had to trust him before he could make his move, but when he made his move, it would be quick. Like a flash.

18

arrie and Rob walked in silence to the car. The sun had nearly set, leaving its pink, purple, and orange finger prints across the sky. The crickets were welcoming the darkness with a serenade.

"Want to get some dinner?" Rob finally asked with a smile.

"Sure." Carrie suddenly realized she was hungry.

Rob drove them to a little restaurant on the outskirts of downtown called Jamaica. The bright pink building stood out among the fast food eateries that lined Broadway, the main drag through the city.

The aroma of Caribbean cuisine filled the small building. A short, man with a thick accent led the pair to a booth in the back of the dimly-lit eatery and handed them their menus. A large aquarium was built into the wall at the end of the table, and brightly-colored fish provided silent entertainment. Reggae music played softly in the background.

It was obvious Rob had been to the eatery often, because he never even opened the menu. Carrie, on the other hand, had never eaten Caribbean cuisine, so when the waiter came to take their order, she was not prepared.

Rob's choice sounded exotic: ox tails with rice and peas, greens, and pineapple punch to wash it all down. Carrie decided on jerk chicken with yellow rice, pineapple sweet potatoes, and iced tea. Once the waiter left with their order, they began rehashing the day's events.

Carrie again relayed the story of Ty and E.J. and felt that they should go back to Fullerton the following day and talk to some more of the neighbors. Rob agreed, noting that they also had more missing children to investigate. They were in the middle of working out a plan for the next day when their food arrived.

They shared tastes of each other's dinner, and ate until they both felt like their stomachs would explode. The food tasted as good as it smelled, and instantly, Carrie was a fan of Caribbean flavor. Once they finished, Rob paid for the meal and they headed out to the car. It was unusually cool for a July evening, so they decided to walk the 10 or so blocks to the parking garage that was housing her vehicle.

Rob was very talkative, telling Carrie about his childhood in North Carolina, his parents' divorce which brought him to Tennessee with his father, and his leaving home at the age of 18. He had been in Nashville for 10 years. His relationship with Harlan began with a chance meeting at the main post office downtown, but that was a story for a different time.

During the course of the conversation, Rob had taken Carrie's hand without her noticing. When she did notice, she flinched, nearly pulling her hand away, only to be met with him tightening his grip and pulling her closer. She did not know why, but for some reason she felt comfortable with this man she had known for a mere 24 hours.

Once they reached her car, and their goodbyes were said, Carrie began the drive back to her apartment. For a big city, the streets were quiet at 10 p.m., which allowed her to spend less time focusing on the traffic, and more time concentrating on the events of the day.

19

Carrie met Rob at his apartment the next morning. He lived on the second floor of an old building in the heart of downtown. The brick and mortar structure sat two blocks from the banks of the Cumberland River, and his apartment took up a third of the second floor. The first floor was inhabited by a music store.

Carrie walked up the wooden steps and knocked on the door of apartment 202. The hallway was dark, with the only light coming from a small window at the end of the hallway. The walls were concrete and in desperate need of a new paint job.

A noise drew her attention, and she turned to see a man lying under the window that faced the river. The rays of sunshine that were actually able to work their way through the dirt-encrusted glass shone on a face covered in a road map of wrinkles that accented sunken-in cheeks and sad eyes. Tangled mops of graying hair were plastered on his forehead and the gray stubble that covered his chin, cheeks, and neck had not seen a razor in weeks.

He coughed again, and took a drink from a liquor bottle, then reached it out toward her as if to offer her a drink. Carrie offered a compassionate smile and shook her head no. The man offered her a toothless smile in return, and pulled the bottle to his chest, cradling it like a baby.

The clicking of the deadbolt startled her back to reality, and suddenly she was face to face with a shirtless Rob.

"Sorry I'm not ready. Come on in and have a seat."

The apartment was small – smaller than hers, if that was possible. It was a typical bachelor pad with posters of action movies and nearly-topless girls covered the walls. One leg of the couch was missing, and where it should have been was a stack of Playboy magazines. A coffee table littered with papers and folders and a t.v. were the only other furniture in the room. The air was filled with the stench of stale beer and Old Spice.

"Nice place you've got here," Carrie said, thinking about how badly the place needed a makeover. Carrie moved an old pizza box out of the way and sat gently on the wobbly couch.

It only took Rob about 10 minutes to finish getting ready. He walked into the living room and looked around. "Sorry about the mess," he commented without attempting to straighten anything up. "I don't usually have people over. In fact, I think you are literally the third person who has ever even been in the apartment."

"How long have you been here?" Carrie asked, standing and walking toward the door.

"About five years." Rob opened the front door and led her out. He locked the door and slammed it shut. "Let's go."

The road to Gallatin was scenic and peaceful. Carrie offered to drive, and decided to avoid the interstate on their way to the small community just north of Nashville.

After driving for 30 minutes, she turned onto Hammond Lane. It was a beautiful, tree-line street leading into the community of Hammond Hill, a subdivision of perfectly-manicured lawns and large houses inhabited by the well to do.

Stephen Bascombe had moved to the neighborhood with his family only two weeks before he disappeared. As Carrie looked at the close-knit neighborhood, she wondered how difficult it must have been for a stranger to come into the area and leave undetected.

"Take a right here on Hammock Way," Rob interrupted her thoughts. He had been reading the police report for most of the drive, and had said little during the drive. "The Bascombes live in the third house on the right, just before the cul-de-sac."

Carrie pulled up to the gated driveway. The house was surrounded by a tall, wrought-iron fence covered in shrubbery, making the house invisible from the street. She pressed the button on a small call box and waited for a response. Rob tapped her on the leg and pointed to a camera strategically placed on top of one of the fence posts.

"May I help you," came a deep voice from the call box.

"My name is Carrie Stevens, and I am investigating the disappearance of Stephen Bascombe. May I come in?"

A long pause was followed by, "This matter has already been discussed. We have nothing more to say." Click.

Carrie looked at Rob, who looked angry. "If I was a parent, and my son was missing, there's no way in hell I wouldn't talk to everyone I could think of if I thought it might help bring him home."

"Unless you have given up hope."

"How can you give up hope when it is your child?" Carrie noticed he was holding the photo of Stephen from the police file.

Their conversation was interrupted by the gate beginning to open. "You may come in," said a woman's voice from the call box.

Carrie drove through the gate and around a driveway which circled a small, grassy patch of lawn that held two benches and a marble statue. The base of the statue sat on a small fountain that supplied water to a small creek that ran around the exterior of the grass island. The yard was actually small compared to the house, which took up most of the acreage. It was a two-story Tudor-style house that looked flawless. Rose bushes lined the front of the dwelling, and granite steps lead visitors to the French doors.

Carrie parked the car. "Wow, talk about money."

"People who live in places like this are making up for something they are lacking." Rob placed the picture back in the file and got out of the car. "They must be lacking a lot."

The pair walked to the door, which opened before they were able to ring the bell. A tall, blonde woman stood before them. She was wearing a cream-colored silk blouse, which was tucked into a pair of brown slacks. Everything about her was perfect. Every hair was perfectly in place, her nails were manicured. The only imperfections were her red, swollen eyes, which told Carrie she was Stephen's mother.

"I apologize for the miscommunication," the woman started, her voice soft and vulnerable, "but my husband is not taking this situation too well." She reached out her hand, "My name is Cynthia Bascombe. Please, please come in." She opened the door wider and stepped back.

Carrie hated walking into unfamiliar houses. To her, it felt like she was in a museum in a foreign country … she never knew what to say or do. The Bascombe home was no exception. They stepped into a stereotypical mansion. The floors were marble and the ceilings high, making it impossible to walk quietly through the house. The door opened into a large foyer with a wide, wooden staircase at the end. Large, expensive-looking pieces of art hung from white walls. Carrie wondered if the house was really a home to Stephen, or more of an intrusion. Could a child be a child in a place like this, she wondered? Cynthia opened a large, wooden door to the right of the front door, and they walked into what could only be described as a sitting room.

It was a large room with two couches and two chairs placed in a circle around a large, round coffee table. The floor was covered with an antique rug. Various small tables holding vases of freshly-cut flowers or family photos were sprinkled throughout the room. Three very large floor to ceiling windows looked out over the side yard.

"You have a beautiful home," Carrie said feeling a little out of her element. She and Rob sat on one of the couches, while Cynthia sat in a chair.

"Thank you. We have only been here for a few weeks. I have to admit, coming from a small farming town that this is not the type of house I ever thought I would be living in."

"I can imagine. I'm from a small town, too."

Rob interjected, "So, do you mind if we ask you some questions about Stephen's disappearance?"

"How rude of me," Cynthia said as she nearly jumped from her seat. "Would you like something to drink? A soda ... water ... coffee?"

"No, thank you," Rob said quickly.

"Yes, I would love a glass of water," Carrie responded. Cynthia nodded and rushed from the room. Carrie leaned toward Rob and whispered, "if we act like we are comfortable here, she might open up more. Right now, she is a nervous wreck." Rob nodded in agreement.

Cynthia returned with a glass and handed it to Carrie. She was also carrying a box of tissues. "My husband will be down in a moment. So, where were we?"

"Tell us a little about Stephen, if you don't mind," Carrie said, taking a sip of her drink.

It was as if the mere mention of her son's name had opened a faucet of tears. She began dabbing at the corner of her eyes with a tissue, her bottom lip trembling. "Stephen, was ... is my angel," she finally said. "We had tried for many years to have a child, but we just couldn't. We had given up hope. Then, one day, I went to the doctor to get a physical for a cruise and found out I was pregnant."

"Wow," Rob piped up, "that must have been some amazing news."

"I couldn't wait to get home and tell Larry. And when he walked through the door, I remember running over, hugging him, and just blurting it out. In 20 years of marriage, that was the only time I had ever seen him cry."

"So, Stephen was your only child?" Carrie inquired.

"No. Larry and I have an older daughter named Sheila. She is 10 years older than Stephen. We always wanted a second child, and we tried for 10 years before Stephen came."

"Is Sheila home today?"

"No, she is in college in Florida. We called her when Stephen went missing, and she wanted to come home, but Larry insisted that she stay down there. No need to impede her education, he said, I didn't agree, but …"

Her story was broken by the appearance of a tall man in a tennis outfit. His gray hair was combed perfectly and he wore a white polo shirt with some sort of reptile sewn on the front. The shirt was tucked into a pair of white shorts complete with belt and pleats. White tube socks and white tennis shoes completed the outfit, and the entire ensemble seemed to accent a tan that was too perfect to be natural.

"Good afternoon," Carrie said standing and offering her hand to shake. The man sauntered over and grasped her hand too tightly.

"Larry Bascombe, and you are?"

"Carrie Stevens. This is my partner, Rob Holton." Rob also rose and shook Larry's hand. Everyone sat back down and endured an uncomfortable silence. Finally, it was broken by Rob.

"So, what is Stephen like? What is his demeanor?"

"Quiet," Cynthia answered. "If we heard him say 10 words a day it was a miracle. He is a good boy. Always woke himself up on time, would be down at the dinner table each morning, homework spread out for inspection, perfectly dressed. His teachers always comment on how polite he is." The thought of her son brought a new round of tears and lip quivering.

"What about extracurricular activities? Does he like sports or anything like that?" Rob asked.

"No," Larry answered so quickly and loudly that it made everyone in the room jump. "He never left that room when he came home from school or on the weekends. I don't know what he was doing up there, but he would not come out."

Another uncomfortable silence filed the room. It was almost suffocating, Carrie thought. The couple was having trouble dealing with the circumstances, that was understandable, but there was something else wrong. Something Carrie could not put her finger on. As they sat there, she was sure she saw Larry shoot a piercing glare or two to his wife, who seemed to be cowering in the chair like a child who was just placed in time out.

"Is Sheila quiet like Stephen?" Carrie inquired.

"No," Larry answered, more subdued. "She is the polar opposite of Stephen. She played softball in high school, got a full ride to the University of Florida. Hell of a pitcher, that girl," Larry's chest started to puff out in pride.

Cynthia added, "We used to joke that the reason Stephen never said much is because he couldn't get a word in when his sister was around. She is very social; loves to be around people. Stephen never seemed to like that. He prefers to be alone."

Suddenly, Larry rose from his chair like a bullet. Cynthia flinched, and then settled herself down, wiping tears with the already-soaked tissue. "I think I have had enough," he said and walked out of the room, slamming the door behind him.

Cynthia looked at the door and then looked at Carrie and Rob with the eyes of a wounded puppy. She excused herself from the room.

"I think we should go," Carrie said, standing. Rob nodded and they left the house.

Once in the car, Rob grabbed the police file and opened it.

"It's amazing that a house that big and beautiful can hold so much darkness and pain," Carrie commented and started the car.

"That house was not built for family; it was built to impress the neighbors. The bricks in that home are held together with arrogance."

Carrie could sense anger from Rob, and she didn't know how to respond.

"Turn right at the end of the driveway. There is a park about two blocks down. That is where Stephen was last seen," Rob said. "Maybe we can find some answers there."

<u>20</u>

Fischer Park was something out of a Thoreau poem. A small pond was lined with various trees that had been there so long their cracked trunks had started turning grey. Carrie wondered how many lovers had kissed in the shade of their long branches, how many secrets had been told there. She wished they could talk and tell what happened to the quiet little boy who disappeared weeks ago.

She pulled into the dirt parking area next to the park. Wooden benches and picnic tables were sprinkled throughout the dark green grass, and most were being used by families out enjoying the beautiful, yet sticky weather. A little boy was sitting on the side of the pond fishing under the careful watch of what appeared to be his big brother. Maybe it was just her imagination, but it seemed like the parents were being more attentive than they probably were with their children on a normal day.

"I'm going to knock on a few doors," Rob said, "if you want, you can walk around the park for a while." He walked away without waiting for an answer. For some reason, this case was bothering him.

Carrie leaned against the hood of the car and took off her sandals. The grass was full and tall, making it perfect for walking barefoot. She began making her way around the pond toward the boys.

"Catch anything?" she inquired when she came within ear shot.

"Not yet," the youngest boy said with a smile, "but we're going to. They got new fish yesterday."

"They fill the pond every week with catfish," the older boy explained without taking his eyes off the younger lad.

Carrie sat down in the grass. "So, either of you know the boy who went missing a few weeks ago?"

"What's it to you?" the older boy asked with a sneer.

"I didn't mean to upset you. My name is Carrie, and I am a reporter. I'm writing a story about the child, and I just wondered if you knew him."

"The *child* has a name."

"I know he does. His name is Stephen. What is your name?" Carrie spoke in a soft voice, hoping to ease the obviously angry young man. He looked like he was about 12 years old. Strands of dirty blonde hair were sticking out from beneath a dirty Atlanta Braves hat that seemed to match his filthy white t-shirt and equally dirty and torn jeans.

"My name is Ryan. I knew Stephen. He was my best friend."

"Mine, too," said the smaller boy, offering a toothless smile.

Ryan put his arm around the boy. "This is my brother, Dougie. He's seven, so everyone is his best friend."

"So, do you remember the day Stephen disappeared?"

"Yeah. We were playing Ninja here in the park."

"Ninja?"

"Yeah, it's a game we made up. One of us would be the Ninja and the other would be the cop looking for him. The Ninja would hide and the cop would search. I guess it's kind of like hide-and-seek, 'cept we are too old to play that, so we play Ninja."

Carrie noticed that Ryan was talking so frankly about his friend. Was it possible that he was over the trauma that quickly, or had he even began worrying? Kids were resilient, Carrie knew that. "So, who was the Ninja the last time you saw Stephen?"

"Stephen was. He was hiding. I looked for a long time, but I couldn't find him. Then the sun started to set. I figured he must have gone home and I just didn't hear him say goodbye. Stephen never would have left without saying goodbye. He didn't talk a lot to people, but he talked to me."

"So, when did you realize he was missing?"

"His mom called and asked my mom if he was at our house. I told mom what happened, and I told her about the blue car ..."

Carrie perked up. "Blue car?"

"Yeah. There was this old, blue car parked on the side of the road. It was weird, because no one ever parked on the road. We were making fun of the car, because it was all rusty and dented. When I was looking for Stephen, I saw the car go down the road. It made me look because it was smoking and I started coughing."

"What did your mom say?"

"She told Stephen's mom, and later she told the policeman who showed up at the house. It was kinda cool when he came. I was hoping the other kids saw him there."

"I appreciate your help, Ryan," Carrie said standing up. She needed to call Rob and look at the police file. Was there any mention of the blue car? She walked away from the pond, looking back just in time to see Dougie reel in a fish.

Stephen wasn't sure why he chose that day to make his move. Maybe it was the way the sun came through the gaps in the walls that morning or the deep orange he could see as the sun set. Maybe he was tired of listening to Thomas cry in the corner. Maybe he wanted freedom so desperately that he was willing to risk his life. Whatever the reason, one thing was clear – he was ready to go home.

"Today is the day," he whispered to Thomas. "If you want to go with me, you better be ready to run."

"B ... but, you could die."

"We could die in here, too. You don't know what his plan is for us. Maybe he is planning to torture and kill us. You don't know." Stephen's fear was making his voice rise. He was starting to tremble, and for a moment, contemplated not doing anything; but something inside him pushed him. Today is the day, he repeated to himself over and over.

Once he heard the footsteps coming down the hall, Stephen crouched in the corner directly across from the door. His heart was racing, his head pounding. He got in a football stance like it was nothing more than a scrimmage in the park and the man entering the room was the quarterback.

The deadbolt clicked and the doorknob began to turn. All sound seemed to be amplified. The door opened, and the outline of the masked man filled the doorway. Three steps in, Stephen thought; count them. One ... ready ... Two ... set ... Three ... go! As the masked man bent down to place the food on the floor, Stephen took off across the floor running as fast as he could. His bare feet made no sound, so the thud of his shoulder striking the man's head was deafening. Stephen heard a loud crack as he sprinted around the man's falling body. He could hear Thomas' feet behind him.

The door opened to a narrow hallway to the right. The boys ran down the hallway, which ended in the living room. Heads of various animals took up the space on every wall in the small room. A fire was crackling in the fireplace; next to that was the door. They flung it open revealing a canvas of blackness in front of him. The two boys ran into the void and found themselves in the midst of a deep forest. The steep, sloping ground made their trip down the mountain a half-run, half-sliding journey.

They ran until their feet and legs were burning and could not hold their bodies anymore. They stopped next to a tree and sat down trying to catch their breath.

"I don't think he is following us," Stephen said between gasps for air.

"I don't either. But he will. He's just going to wait until the sun comes up."

"We'll be so far away from here by then that he will never find us."

"I hope you are right," Thomas said before bursting in tears again. Stephen contemplated just leaving the boy, but knew that was wrong. They got out together, and they were going to be saved together.

The man opened his eyes. The taste of blood filled his mouth. His body was numb, and it wasn't until he tried to stand that he realized the dire situation he was faced with: he was not able to move.

The mask was suffocating, though it was not stopping any air from entering his lungs. Though he knew this could be the end for him, a sensation of relief came over his body. This nightmare he had been living for months was coming to an end. He never wanted to be in the little cabin with the terrified, crying children. He had a duty to family, and finally, that duty
was over. He could not stop the smile from forming on his lips as he drifted slowly into unconsciousness.

21

C arrie and Rob were sitting on the floor in Carrie's apartment pouring over police reports and interviews. Carrie had prepared a quick meal of Cashew Chicken and fried rice, and since there was only one chair at her makeshift table, they were sitting on the floor reading as they ate. Chinese was one of the few meals Carrie was able to cook well.

Careful not to soil the paperwork, they looked for references to the mysterious blue car, and found none. Not even the interview with Ryan or his mother mentioned the car, though both had claimed the police were told. By the time they had finished eating, every piece of paper had been scanned, and their frustration had risen to new levels.

"How could they miss this?" Carrie thought out loud.

"Maybe they didn't miss it. Maybe it was intentionally left out," Rob answered stretching his legs out and leaning back on his outstretched arms.

Carrie took his cue and stood, stretching her back and legs before picking up the dirty dinner plates and carrying them to the kitchen. "Why would they leave something out? Won't that just make their ability to solve the case even more difficult?"

"If their intention is to solve the cases, then yes, it would make it more difficult. But, what if it is not their intention to solve the cases?"

Carrie stopped washing one of the plates and stared at the wall. "Why wouldn't they want to solve the cases, Rob? That makes no sense."

Rob stood up and walked to the kitchen and leaned against the door frame. "Well, let's think hypothetically. All of these kids are missing, and the police are clueless. They have no suspects, no motives, no witnesses, no weapons, no bodies … nothing. Not only are they frustrated, but they are also embarrassed."

"Ok, but why hide the little evidence they do have?" Carrie opened the door to the refrigerator, pulled out two cans of Coke, and handed one to Rob. He followed her into the living room where they tiptoed through the mess on the floor and plopped down on the couch.

He continued, "Well, the public wants answers that the police can't provide. The newspapers are sniffing around; CNN has been parked in front of the Sheriff's Office for a week. Now they have this smoking gun that they can't tie to anything. If they are coming up empty, why not just omit the evidence and try to save a little face than include it and look like the Keystone cops?"

Carrie sat back on the couch and closed her eyes. She hated to admit that what Rob was saying made sense, but she refused to believe that people would do something like that. These officers had sworn to protect the community. If Rob was right, all they were protecting was their collective asses. "So, what if you are wrong?" she finally asked.

"Right or wrong, we have to find out about that blue car."

"I agree. So, what is our next move?"

Rob leaned forward, placed his soda can on the floor, and ran his fingers through his hair. "Well, you mentioned going back and talking to E.J.'s brother ... what was his name?"

"Ty."

"Right. Why don't you head over there tomorrow morning and sniff around. I'll go to the Police Department and the Sheriff's Office and see what I find. We can meet at my apartment around noon, eat some lunch, and figure out what to do next."

"Sounds like a plan."

Sighing, Rob looked at the mess on the floor and then at the clock: 9:45. "I have got to get home and get some rest. You want me to help pick up?"

"Nah, I'll get it."

Rob rose from the couch and followed Carrie to the door. She opened it for him and smiled.

"You did a good job today," he said before leaning over and giving her a quick kiss on the lips. "See you tomorrow."

Carrie fought the urge to grab him by the arm, pull him back into the apartment, and make love with him on the floor. Instead, she closed the door and leaned up against it. For the first time in her life, things seemed to be going perfectly.

She made her way into the living room and began putting the paperwork back into their respective files. Once she finished, she headed to the bedroom and turned on her computer. She knew sleep would elude her, so she decided to get some research done, and she started with the one person who creeped her out the most – Larry Bascombe.

A quick Google search turned up a total of 15 newspaper articles. Mr. Bascombe was a very successful businessman in the New Orleans area. His construction company, SBI, was founded in the early 90s by Spencer Bascombe, Larry's father. The company had landed some good jobs over the early years, but nothing major. In January, 1999, Spencer Bascombe passed away in an automobile accident, and SBI was then taken over by his sons, Larry and Gerald.

Gerald was the older of the two brothers, and the least interested in running a business it seemed. Another Google search showed that Gerald had been living in the Houston area with his wife and two daughters. He was 45 when his father passed, and was running a successful magazine in Texas. As reluctant as he apparently was at getting involved with the family business, he also knew there was a chance to earn some big money, so he became a silent partner and let his younger brother do all the work.

Public records showed that Larry worked hard, and two years after inheriting the business, he was able to land a multi-million dollar contract with the government to build several federal courthouses in Louisiana, Alabama, and Tennessee. That explained the move to Nashville.

One article showed that Larry was a generous man. When Hurricane Katrina devastated the Gulf coast, SBI had been instrumental in helping several neighborhoods rebuild in the aftermath. In fact, in 2007 he had been named businessman of the year by the New Orleans Chamber of Commerce.

Carrie pulled up the article about his award, and stared at the picture attached. Larry Bascombe was surrounded by the mayor of New Orleans, the governor of Louisiana, and had a woman hanging on his arm, but that woman was not his wife Cynthia. The caption identified the woman as Patrice Bascombe, Larry's wife.

Intrigued, Carrie did a public records search and discovered that Patrice and Larry Bascombe had divorced six months after the picture was taken. A month later, Larry married his current wife. It took a moment for the information to register, but when it did, it hit Carrie like a freight train. Stephen Bascombe was not Cynthia's son. So, why had she lied?

Carrie closed the laptop and set it beside her on the bed. She knew tomorrow morning was going to take her back to the Bascombe's for some answers.

22

Consciousness was becoming a struggle for the man. The slightest bit of exertion would either tire him out or cause him to pass out. He had reached the point of giving up, when a set of lights shined through the cracks in the wall.

The dark truck pulled to a stop in front of the cabin's open door. The driver grabbed the shotgun from under the seat and slowly headed for the cabin. The dark sky was beginning to turn to light, so vision was not impossible at this point.

The man struggled to remain conscious. He tried as hard as he could to push the air out of his lungs and make a noise, but nothing happened. He focused on the footsteps on the other side of the house, and prayed that they would make their way to him.

The soft light from outside was just enough for the driver to maneuver through the living room area and toward the hallway. The shotgun provided courage where there was none, and soft steps provided security as the driver headed down the dark hall to the back of the house.

The man opened his eyes and tried to make the blurriness disappear. He tried to keep his vision on the doorway in hopes of seeing his savior enter.

The door on the right was secure. The deadbolt was hanging as it should. A gloved hand reached out and tugged on it to make sure it was locked; it was. The door on the left was cracked open. The metal barrel of the shotgun made a scraping sound as it pushed the wooden door open. Frightened eyes came in contact with eyes on the verge of death. The shotgun fell to the floor.

E.J. heard the footsteps, but they were different this time. The Boogeyman was loud and liked to scare him. This was not the boogeyman. He curled himself up into a tight ball in the corner of the room and wished Ty was there to protect him.

23

Carrie spent most of the morning reviewing the files to make sure nothing was missed concerning either the blue car or Stephen Bascombe. She knew they had been careful the night before, but so many things seemed to be wrong.

She took a long shower to get her thoughts in order and to practice what she was going to say to Cynthia and Tom. Part of her wanted to call Rob and inform him of her newly-discovered information, but the other part of her wanted to prove that she was capable of investigating on her own. She stood in the shower until the hot water ran out, quickly got dressed, and ate a light breakfast. It was a long drive to Gallatin, and she wanted to get a fairly early start.

Traffic was light on the interstate, but that was not unusual for a Monday morning. The drive to the Bascombe home was considerably shorter than the previous time. This time, when she pulled up to the iron gate, it was open and a large moving truck was sitting in the driveway. Carrie parked beside the truck and made her way to the front door where two large men were carrying out a couch.

"Excuse me," Carrie said. "Do you know where I might find Mr. or Mrs. Bascombe?"

The moving man who was walking backwards called for his partner to stop, and they slowly set the couch down on the walkway. "Yo, Buck," he called to his friend, "Where's that lady?"

"Upstairs. We gonna move this thing or stand around jabbering?"

The man looked at Carrie and nodded toward the house. "There you go, lady." He bent over and picked up the couch with a grunt before making his way toward the truck.

As she quietly made her way across the granite floor, Carrie was glad she had chosen to wear sneakers that morning. She walked slowly up the stairs and once at the top, she was faced with a long hallway. In total, there were six doors, three on each side, and all of them were open. Carrie adjusted her baseball cap, straightened her ponytail, tucked in her Tennessee Titans t-shirt and began making her way down the hallway.

"Mother, it's over. You know that. Quit playing this game and move on. It's not worth the heartache anymore." The voice was stern and not one Carrie knew. She wondered if maybe it was the daughter the couple had spoken of during the interview.

Carrie walked slowly down the hall toward the voices. When she approached the last room on the right, she stopped. The sound of sobbing was much louder now, and was diminished only by the shuffling of feet across carpet.

"I ... just ... can't believe ... he ...he's gone," Cynthia worked out between sniffles. Carrie felt awkward just standing there and decided to knock softly on the room's doorframe. An unfamiliar face peered around the corner.

"Hi, my name is Carrie and I was here the other day. I was hoping to speak to Mrs. Bascombe."

"As you can tell, this is not a good time." The woman stepped out into the hallway and closed the door behind her. "My name is Sheila, and you are?" She was an attractive woman in her early 20s. Her hair was short and messy with strands wet with sweat lying on her forehead. She wore a pastel green t-shirt with the name of a college bar plastered across the front, khaki cargo shorts and flip flops that revealed painted toenails and two toe rings on her right foot.

"Carrie Stevens. Nice to meet you. I hate to be nosey, but what is going on here?"

"Mother and Larry have decided to take a hiatus from each other. She will be moving in with me in Florida for a while."

"That seems so sudden. I was just here and everything seemed to be ok. Will Mr. Bascombe be staying in here?" Carrie immediately realized she had touched on a sore spot as the anger on Sheila's face grew. The young woman's fists were clenched, and she looked like she was struggling to remain cordial and in control.

"Larry will ... has ... moved back to the New Orleans area to spend some much needed time with his first wife. If you would like to speak with him, I'm sure he would be more than willing to gain some media attention and speak with you with the cameras rolling, of course."

"But I just spoke with them both yesterday."

"As you can see, things move quickly in this household. Now, if you will excuse me."

"Sheila, wait," Carrie pleaded. "Just one more question."

The daughter turned around and quickly wiped a tear from her eye to hide any sign that she was emotional over the events. "What?'

Carrie pulled out a piece of paper with the picture she had found of Larry online. "Is this his first wife," she asked, handing the paper to Sheila.

Sheila stared at the paper, her fists quickly beginning to ball up. Without a word, she tore the picture into small pieces, opened the door to the bedroom and disappeared inside, leaving Carrie wading in a sea of confusion in the hallway. She let herself out of the house and to her car, where she sat for what seemed like hours.

Was it possible for a family to break up that quickly? What about Stephen? Had they given up on him?

Carrie started the car and stopped at the end of the driveway. Just as she was about to turn onto the road, she felt strange; as if someone were watching her. Just as she looked to her left, a man with a very familiar face raced by in a black sports car. Carrie contemplated, just for a moment, whether to follow the vehicle, but thought better and squinted to read the license plate; it was a move that proved to be impossible.

24

Somehow, the two boys fell asleep despite the strange noises and rustling leaves that seemed determined to keep them awake. Stephen awoke when the sun's rays worked themselves through the clutter of the pine tree branches and landed on his face, warming his cheeks and slowly opening his eyes with their brightness.

He sat up and looked around. Dense forest blanketed the horizon, and suddenly his adolescent fear of the captor was replaced with a grown-up fear of survival. How were the boys going to eat? Where would they find water? Would they make it out alive? His thoughts were interrupted by the sound of Thomas turning over in the leaves.

The boys said nothing to each other, but their eyes spoke volumes. Stephen was the leader – a role he was more that capable of handling. He stood up and began walking down the mountain some more, the crunching of leaves let him know that Thomas was not far behind. Behind the boys, in the distance, smoke rose from the cabin chimney.

The shotgun hitting the floor was the sound of relief for the man. He could not look up at the figure before him, but he could see the outline of knees next to him. If the gloved hands were touching him, he could not tell. He hoped they were.

"It'll be alright," said the voice through the darkness. The man closed his eyes and said a silent prayer of thanks.

25

arrie called Rob's cell phone, but there was no answer. That seemed to be the story of her life at that moment – a lot of questions with no answers. She left him a message and headed to Fullerton and another conversation with Ty.

The neighborhood was the same as it was two days ago – quiet. Carrie pulled up to the park area and parked her car in the exact spot she did the last time. The only difference this day was the missing group of young men that had given her such a hard time earlier.

Carrie had written Ty's address down and pulled out a city map. Fuller Park was surrounded by four streets – Smith Street, on the north side, was Ty's. Carrie folded the map and got out of the car.

Her journey across the park was quick. She did not want any altercations. Once she was on Smith Street, it did not take her long to find the house. Like the others on the street, it was small and run-down. There were sporadic spots of grass in the tiny yard, the rest covered in dirt. A large oak tree with three folding chairs and a card table beneath its massive limbs sat next to the road. There were no cars in sight, but an old 10-speed bicycle was leaning against the house.

Carrie walked up to the front of the home. The front door was open and a wooden frame with torn screens blocked entrance into the house. She knocked on the doorframe.

Ty came from the back of the house and stopped when he saw who it was. He wiped his hands with a dish towel and opened the screen door. He was shirtless and wearing a pair of dark-blue work pants.

"I wanted to ask you a few more questions," Carrie said with a smile.

"I gotta be at work at noon."

"This won't take long, I promise."

After a moment of hesitation, he nodded his head to invite her in and walked to the back of the house again. Carrie walked into the living room. The smallness of the room compounded with the stench of human waste and dirt slapped her face and took her breath away.

The room held a large couch with ripped fabric. The corners were chewed indicating there was some animal in the house. The couch and floor were littered with clothes and trash. Across from the couch sat a small table and two wooden chairs. Plates and bowls on the table were crawling with roaches, and flies were buzzing around the rotting food. The place was not fit to be lived in, especially by a child, but what other choice was there? Carrie fought the urge to start picking up the mess, and sat timidly on the couch.

Ty came back in the room dressed in a fast-food uniform stained with grease and sat down on one of the chairs facing Carrie. He busied himself with putting on his shoes, and offered no apologies for the mess.

"So, Ty," Carrie began, "I have a question about the day E.J. disappeared."

"Figured you did," he said without looking up. "I mean, why else would you be here?"

"In interviewing family and friends of other missing children in the area, one person mentioned seeing a blue car that didn't seem to belong drive away from the scene just after the boy disappeared. Do you remember anything like that?"

"Can't says I do."

"What about any strangers in the area at the time. Do you recall seeing anyone who didn't belong?"

Ty finished messing with his shoes and looked at Carrie, a wave of anger crossing his face. "In this neighborhood, everyone looks like they don't belong. Look, lady. I done told you what I know. I was playing basketball, he was playing with his toys, and the next thing I knew he was gone. Vanished. I didn't see no more. Why can't you people believe me?" By the end of his statement, his anger flashed across his eyes and was quickly washed away by frustration. He buried his face in his hands and began sobbing, his shoulders shaking.

"I believe you," Carrie said, struggling to fight her own tears. Not knowing what to say, Carrie stood and let herself out of the house.

She put on her sunglasses and decided to question some of the neighbors. She was confident Rob had not contacted anyone on Ty's street when they were here before.

Carrie knocked on doors without a response and was about to give up and head to the car when an older lady approached her.

"Are you that reporter lady?" She looked to be in her 70s. Her dark skin brought out the grey in her hair and highlighted the canyons of wrinkles that seemed to cover every inch of her face. A long housecoat covered her bent body, and she teetered on a wooden cane.

"Yes, ma'am, I am. And you are?"

"Georgia Washington Lincoln Kinsey Hoverton," the woman responded proudly with a smile. She reached out an ancient hand and shook the young reporter's.

"I'm Carrie Stephens."

"Yes, well, Miss Carrie, come with me." Georgia turned and hobbled down the street, favoring her right hip. Curious, Carrie followed.

Not a word was spoken during the walk that took much longer than it should have. The old woman stopped in front of each home and looked, like a policeman on patrol, before finally making her way up the dusty walkway of a lime green house at the end of the street. She sat down hard on a worn lawn chair placed on the porch next to the dirty front door and used the end of her cane to pull another lawn chair across from her.

Carrie sat down and was treated to a glass of warm lemonade poured from a pitcher sitting on the floor next to Georgia's chair.

Carrie noticed that the entire neighborhood was visible from the porch, and she was soon aware that Mrs. Hoverton spent most of her day watching the world pass by in front of her. The old woman took a long, slow drink of the lemonade before speaking in a thick, Southern drawl. "You know, I have lived in this neighborhood for fifty years."

"Really?"

"Yes, Miss Carrie. My husband Orville and I were one of the first couples to buy a house here. Times have changed things, though. This area used to be ripe with scenery. Green grass everywhere; soft grass. The kind you could lay down on in the heat of the summer and feel like it was swallowing you. We used to go sit under the oak tree in the park, before it was a park, of course. My chil'ren played in that park. They didn't need no video games, or cell phones. They would be cops or robbers, cowboys or Indians. Their imaginations ran wild, and so did they. From morning to dinner time, I didn't even see my chil'ren during the summer. Their grandkids are too afraid to play there, now."

Georgia sat back in her chair and took a sip of the lemonade. She was lost in her world of memories, each one bringing a smile to her face. Then came the solemnness; the seriousness that seemed to make her body tense and the frown lines cut across her forehead.

"I used to watch those chil'ren play, Tyrone and his brother. They are the good kids. They never got into trouble, never said a coarse word. It was always 'yes ma'am' and 'no ma'am.' When their aunt went away, I offered to help Tyrone. I offered him a place to stay, food to eat. Boy like him don't need to be worrying about where their next meal is going to come from; but he wouldn't have anything to do with it. He was determined to make it on his own. That damn woman."

"Who?"

"That so-called aunt of theirs. She knew she wouldn't be able to handle raising them. She never should have taken them in. But she did, and her drugs were more important than those kids. Now look at them. It's a damn shame. I remember the day the police car showed up at her house. Big, white police
officer brought her out a few minutes later in handcuffs. She weren't crying … it was like she was waiting for the anvil to drop on her head, and when it did, she actually looked a little relieved." The old woman pointed a shaky finger at Ty's house. "I waited there for hours, and when that boy showed up, I told him what happened, offered him a place to stay. He said no."

Carrie sat back in her seat trying to take it all in. All she could do was feel sorry for the teen. Her thoughts were broken by Georgia.

"When E.J. disappeared, the whole neighborhood was in shock. We know there are bad seeds out there, but not here; not in our neighborhood. Every family was out there trying to find that boy, and when the police showed up, they questioned a few of us, but you could tell they wasn't worried; just another missing black boy on the bad side of town."

"Did you happen to see a blue car in the neighborhood? One that you had never seen before?"

Georgia closed her eyes for a moment and thought. "Now that you mention it, there was a bit of commotion when this old, dented blue car backfired over there on Fuller Street," her story was interrupted by her breaking into laughter. "Edna, the uptight old lady who lives in that corner house over there, well she about peed her pants. Why, she walked down to the road and started screaming something awful. It was hilarious."

"Did anyone tell the police about this?"

"Sweetie, we told the police everything we knew. Problem was they weren't listening. Half the stuff we said weren't even written down."

Carrie sat in silence. At least two people had seen what appeared to be the same vehicle, yet there was no mention of the car in any of the police reports. Something wasn't right.

After finishing her drink and thanking Georgia for her time, Carrie made her way back to her car and tried to call Rob again. He finally answered, and they agreed to meet to share news.

26

Centennial Park sat just outside of downtown Nashville and was one of the city's largest. The park housed numerous trees and picnic tables, and, uniquely, a replica of the Greek Parthenon. The beauty of the place always amazed Carrie, and she spent many a weekend in college sitting under the large oaks pondering topics for papers or studying for tests, but when she arrived to meet Rob, the beauty was overshadowed by the realization that there could be a darker element lurking within. Somewhere in this park could be the next missing child, and any one of the people enjoying time with their families, sitting and reading books under the massive trees, or picnicking with their significant others could be the monster that has been terrorizing the city.

Carrie found an empty bench facing the Parthenon and waited for Rob. About 50 feet in front of her, a man and his pet squirrel were drawing the attention of the children in the park. The man was squatting with the squirrel sitting on his knee and he was feeding it peanuts. The animal seemed to have little to no fear of humans, as the children were able to pet its head and offer it food. She couldn't help but smile at the sight, and was so entranced by the sight that she did not even notice that Rob had arrived and had eased his way quietly on the bench.

"He's pretty cool huh?" he said, causing Carrie to jump.

"You scared the shit out of me, jerk," she said smiling while punching him in the arm. To her relief, he smiled back.

"That guy's name is Yuri, and his squirrel's name is Thumper."

"You know him?"

Rob leaned forward and placed his elbows on his knees, trying to get a closer look at the man and his pet. His hair was haphazardly stuffed into a baseball cap, and, despite the heat, he was wearing jeans and a polo shirt. Pools of sweat were starting to soak through the fabric at his chest and make dark circles on his shirt. "I don't know him personally, but I know of him. A friend of mine used to come to this park every day and sit for hours. One day Yuri showed up and started talking to him."

Carrie smiled. "That was a nice gesture. I bet your friend really appreciated the conversation."

Rob's face turned serious and his eyes grew distant. "Yeah ... that damn squirrel was all my friend talked about for a long, long time. It was the highlight of his day. You could always tell the days it was raining or when Yuri didn't show up to the park. My friend would go into a depression. He'd cut himself off from the world and just kind of lay there like a lump on the couch."

Carrie didn't know how to respond, and Rob seemed to pick up on her confusion. "My friend was battling some bad, bad demons. There was something about that squirrel that made his demons go away, if even for just an hour."

"Does your friend still come to the park?"

Rob looked at the ground. "No. He's in prison now," he said, looking at her through moist eyes. "But, that's a story for another day."

He stood up and stretched, turned to Carrie and smiled. "So, what happened today?"

Back to business, Carrie told Rob about her trip to the Bascombe house and about the information she discovered during her internet search. Rob suggested they find out more about Larry's first wife, "even if we have to drive down there and confront her in person." Then came the news about the blue car.

"Georgia, a neighbor of Ty's said she noticed the blue car because of a commotion. Apparently the car backfired and scared a cantankerous woman near the park. She wasn't able to see who was in the car, but I bet the other woman got a good look. I think we should find that woman, but I don't like going over there by myself."

"Why don't we head over there this afternoon? Right now, I think we need to get with Harlan. I've spent all morning at the Sheriff's Office trying to talk to someone associated with this case, and no one will give me the time of day."

The thought of having to meet with Harlan again made Carrie sick to her stomach, but solving this case was the most important thing, and she was willing to do whatever it took.

They both rose from the bench and walked, hand in hand, to Rob's car, deciding to leave Carrie's at the park for the time being. Harlan's office was not far from the park, but was too far to walk.

Once they arrived, they found themselves yet again sitting and listening to elevator music in the stuffy waiting room of his office. Harlan finally gave the ok for them to come to his office after a 30 minute time span.

Carrie and Rob explained what they knew so far, and Rob mentioned the trouble he was having at the Sheriff's Office. That piece of news seemed to irritate Harlan, and he picked up the phone, dialed some numbers, and pushed a button which turned on the speakerphone. After three rings, a familiar voice came over the line.

"Jimmy Tate, how can I help you," said the sheriff.

"Jimmy, it's Harlan."

"Well hey there, Harlan, what can I do you for?" Carrie shivered as the sheriff's deep, country accent crawled up her spine.

"I have a problem, Tate. Seems my investigator is trying to get some information from some of your deputies, and they aren't cooperating." Harlan leaned back in his leather chair and interlocked his fingers behind his head. The buttons of his shirt struggled to keep in his stomach. "Now, I thought we had your full cooperation on this matter."

"You have my full cooperation, Harlan, but I cannot force my investigators to offer up any evidence they feel could compromise the investigation. That's just the way it has to be."

Harlan's face grew red, and he leaned close to the phone. "You listen to me, Tate. We talked long and hard about the ramifications of this investigation and of my anticipation concerning its outcome. You are throwing roadblocks in my road to the governor's mansion, and I promise you, I have the power to eliminate those problems, and your job if necessary." Rage had turned Harlan's voice to a hiss.

"You can threaten me and my job all you want, but the fact of the matter is it won't change a damn thing. Evidence is evidence. Now, if you want to send your little investigators over here, I will sit down with them and offer them as much as I can. Let's see what we come up with, and then you can get back up on your horse and start making your ride into the sunset. Sound good to you?" Carrie could tell from his voice that the sheriff was smiling.

Harlan picked up the receiver and turned his back to Carrie and Rob. He was talking too low for the duo to hear what he was saying, but they had a pretty good idea that the language was harsh. Once he finished with the conversation, he swiveled around and revealed a crimson face covered in sweat.

"You two need to go over to the Sheriff's Office right now and talk to Mr. Tate. He has assured me he will provide you with any information you need to continue your investigation. If there are any more problems, contact me." He reached into his pocket and retrieved two business cards. "My cell phone number is on the back."

The Davidson County Sheriff's Office took up an entire city block on the banks of the Cumberland River just north of downtown. The building was in desperate need of a makeover, and looked every minute of its 50 years. Carrie and Rob made their way up the concrete steps to the front door and through the metal detector just inside. They told the receptionist they needed to speak to Sheriff Tate and were directed to his office on the second floor.

A short ride in a creaky elevator brought them to the second floor which was basically a long hallway with offices on each side. A plastic sign in front of them informed them that Tate's office was to the right. They made their way down the hall and found his space at the end.

An older woman was sitting in the foyer of the office. Her outdated clothing and unkempt hair made the secretary look frumpy. She inquired why they were there and used a tired voice to direct them to two folding chairs across the room. They were not there long before they were sent to the sheriff's office.

Sheriff Tate's office looked like a broom closet compared to Harlan's. Jimmy sat behind a small metal desk covered in paper work. Filing cabinets lined on each wall covered up any pictures or degree he might want to display. There was only one other seat in the space, and Carrie sat down at Rob's insistence.

"So, you all are Harlan's team, huh," the Sheriff said with a smile. He looked at Carrie and continued, "I remember you from the council meetings."

Carrie held out her hand. "Carrie Stevens." Rob followed with his own handshake and introduction.

The sheriff sat back in his chair and put a cigar in his mouth without lighting it. "Look, kids. I want to help you. No one wants to solve this case more than I do, but I am limited by the law as to what I can offer you evidence-wise. Harlan doesn't understand that. I hope you do."

"I only have one problem, Sheriff," Rob began. He explained the missing information on the blue car from the police reports, and the sheriff seemed to be genuinely concerned about this piece of information. He jotted down some notes on a legal pad as Rob spoke, noting names of the witnesses and what they said. Once he finished talking, the Sheriff sat back in his seat.

"I will be getting to the bottom of this, I assure you. I will not tolerate incompetence from any of my employees. I will speak to the lead investigator on this case and will take whatever action is necessary to assure this won't happen again."

"I appreciate that, Sheriff," Rob responded with a smile.

"Tell you what. If you need information, you come to me, and I will personally get you what I can to help you out."

Rob and Carrie thanked the Sheriff and headed out of the building. "I think that went well," Rob said with a smile.

"Me, too."

They started walking back to Rob's car, when the smell of barbecue drew their attention and made Carrie's stomach begin to rumble. Without saying a word, Rob took her hand and led her to the source of the aroma, a restaurant called "Bill's Barbecue."

It was a small establishment with a total of seven picnic tables. Three were occupied by business couples. Carrie and Rob walked across a brick floor to a table in the back and sat. The walls were wooden and covered in sports posters from every sport imaginable. A shelf sat above the wall that kept the kitchen hidden from the dining room and was filled with football helmets and pictures.

A waitress carrying two menus smiled a nearly toothless smile and used a thick Georgia accent to introduce herself as Mabel. A bandana kept her hair pulled back from her forehead. She wore a Bill's B-B-Q shirt and jeans that were about two sizes too small. Once the drink orders were taken, she lumbered to the kitchen.

Carrie decided on a pulled pork dinner and Rob wanted ribs. Once their drinks were brought and their orders taken, they began to talk about the case and their next move.

"I really think we need to head back to E.J.'s neighborhood and talk to the neighbors. Chances are if Georgia saw as much as she did, then other people may have, too," Carrie said.

"And there was also that lady. The one she said was startled by the backfire. She was close enough that she may have seen his face."

"Sounds like we definitely need to head back there."

Their conversation was interrupted by their waitress delivering their food. Carrie took a bite of her pulled pork and felt an explosion of taste erupt in her mouth. It was the best barbecue she'd ever had. They two ate in silence for minutes before Rob finally spoke.

"We are forgetting something very important, though."

Carrie cocked her head to the side. "What?"

"There are two other missing children that we haven't even looked at yet: Johnson Pickering and Landon Rodriguez. Maybe we should investigate those two and see if there are any similarities to the other missing kids before we dig any deeper."

She looked up and couldn't help but smile. Rob's face and fingers were covered in barbecue sauce. He noticed her looking and offered a sheepish grin. "Guess I'm kind of a messy eater."

<u>27</u>

Two days of hiking left the boys tired and hungry. They were just about to sit down to rest yet again when Stephen heard a welcoming sound – running water. Without saying a word, he began running, and minutes later and they were staring at a river.

Both boys fell to their knees on the shore and drank as fast and their hands could shovel the cool liquid into their mouths. For Stephen it was a sign of life that was much needed for his personal morale; for Thomas, it ran much deeper than that and took him to a happier time and place. He remembered a trip with his mother, one of the few they ever took, and a stop along the roadside where they waded into the flowing brook and gathered river rocks. He could remember running his hands over the smooth stones and the broad smile his mother gave him as she helped him search for those natural treasures.

Stephen sat down on the river bank and looked up through the trees as the sun sent rays of hope through the branches of the tall pine trees.

"I think we should follow the river. Right or left, either way, we are bound to find someone who can help us." He thought about the times his father took him camping; there was always a river or lake nearby so they could fish for their dinner.

Thomas shook his head yes, and wiped the streaks of memories that were running down his cheeks. He looked down in the water and picked up a small, smooth stone and placed it in his pocket.

Dane knew there really was no way they were going to find the boys. The woods were thick and ran for miles in any direction; not to mention the bears and wildcats that lived in the area. Chances were good that the boys were going to be eaten or die of starvation. He dare not say that aloud, though. In this family, punishment was swift and hard.

The truck rolled to a stop deep in the forest, and the driver got out and headed to the bed of the vehicle. Every movement made Dane's head throb. He opened the door and gingerly made his way to the back of the truck. A rifle was thrust into his hand, and the two headed into the woods in search of their prey.

<u>28</u>

The Green Hills section of Nashville sat on the west side of downtown, and was a pattern of tree-lined roads and old, Victorian-style mansions with vines crawling up the walls.

Garrett Kauffman Memorial Park sat in the middle of a sleepy neighborhood and was busy with children playing in its lush, manicured grass. Oak trees shaded nearly every inch of the park, which easily covered 200 acres; a duck pond sat in the middle.

Rob pulled the car into a gravel parking area and turned off the engine. "Going door to door is going to be an adventure. If we are even able to get past the maids and butlers, there is little chance the families will even bother to talk to us."

"Maybe we should skip the door-to-door for now and just hit Johnson Pickering's home. Maybe the family will be able to lead us to more witnesses," Carrie responded.

Rob consulted his map and looked around. "His house was on Maple Road, which is the one on the other side of the park. Considering the heat, I'd rather drive over there than walk."

"Agreed."

Rob started the car and drove around the park, turning onto Maple Road. The Pickering resident was a large two-story home facing the park. Rob parked on the street in front of the house and got out, taking off his glasses to get a better look at the residence. "Wow," was all he could muster.

Wow was right. The house sat on a large piece of land and was accented by a perfectly-cut lawn and hedges, a large swimming pool, a tennis court, and what appeared to be a pool house or mother-in-law apartment at the back of the property.

Carrie and Rob walked up the driveway, noting the late-model BMW car and Mercedes SUV sitting near the home. Once they reached the door, Carrie knocked. They stood in an uncomfortable silence until a click of the deadbolt drew their attention.

The door opened slowly and revealed an older, black woman in a stereotypical maid's uniform. "May I help you?"

Rob stuck out his hand. "Good afternoon, my name is Rob and this is Carrie and we are investigating the disappearance of Johnson. Are his parents home?"

Without saying a word, the maid turned and walked away, leaving the door open. Rob stepped into the home, grabbed Carrie's hand and pulled her in behind him.

The inside of the home was just as plush as the outside. An oriental rug sat in the middle of the foyer, and the door faced two sets of stairs heading to the second floor. Red carpet was everywhere visible, and it was accented by floral wallpaper. Unlike the Bascombe home, this place was comforting.

Carrie's eyes were drawn to an antique drop leaf desk covered with framed family photos. The picture in the middle showed a young couple with three children and an older woman. The only boy child looked happy. He was smiling a big, toothy smile and was leaning slightly toward the younger woman who was apparently his mother. The sound of footsteps coming down the carpeted stairs drew her attention.

The woman in the photo, though now a little older, smiled as she approached the foyer. "Hi, my name is Linda Pickering. How can I help you?"

Carrie introduced herself and Rob and explained their reasons for visiting. "We are trying to find out as much information as possible about Johnson and what may have happened."

The woman's face went from cheerful to serious. She smoothed her pink cotton shirt, and tugged at the bottom of it. "Why don't we step out onto the patio to talk? It's a beautiful day." Carrie found that to be an odd statement considering the mercury was nearing 100 in the shade. Linda turned and opened a door, revealing a long hallway. "This way," the woman said softly and headed down the hall. The smell of fresh-baked bread weaved its way out of the doorway. As they walked toward a doorway leading outside, Carrie noticed that a doorway on the right lead to the kitchen.

The back porch sat between the house and a large, sectioned swimming pool that was separated by rocks and flora with a small waterfall in the middle. The porch ran the length of the home, and was covered with a roll-away awning. A wooden table with a glass top, and four matching chairs sat just outside the back door. Linda picked a chair facing the home and Rob and Carrie sat facing toward the pool.

"Johnson … John … is my oldest child. He was 13 when he disappeared." Linda clasped her hands on the table, and Carrie noticed her knuckles were starting to turn white.

"What can you tell us about the day he disappeared?" Rob asked softly.

Linda's eyes started to tear up as she struggled to keep her emotions in check. "We had an argument that morning. Not a big one, but an argument none the less. He's a teenager. You can imagine how difficult that can be on a parent at times."

"Absolutely," Carrie said.

"So, when he didn't come home that afternoon, I assumed he was making me pay for my strictness by running away."

"Had he run away in the past?"

"No. He had threatened it many times, but he never followed through."

"May I ask what the argument was about," Rob asked.

Before she could answer, the maid showed up carrying a tray carrying a pitcher of iced tea and three glasses. She set the tray gently on the table, poured the tea, and set a glass in front of each person. "Thank you Anita," Linda said with a smile that indicated the maid needed to leave. She got the hint and left quickly.

"She's been with us for years; practically raised John. I was a teacher when John was born and kept teaching for the first year until I got pregnant again. Kevin, my husband, wanted me to give up my career and become a full-time mom, so I did. Best move I ever made."

"I bet your kids appreciated it," Carrie offered with a smile.

"They did, for the most part. But, you know how it can get when Mom is home all the time. Kids start rebelling, and John was no different than any other child. He liked to test my limits. When Tina, our second child came, John was jealous. He started to cling to Anita, turning to her for motherly attention, and she was more than happy to give it to him when needed; not that I minded. Having two small children around is stressful." Linda picked up her glass and took a long, thoughtful drink.

"So, what limits was John testing the day he disappeared?" Carrie asked.

"We, John's father and I, were upset over John's unwillingness to do his chores around the house. We are obviously ok money-wise, and we do have help around here, but we still expect the children to do their fair share of work around the house. My husband, Phil, works hard for us to live this lifestyle, and we refuse to allow our children to take it for granted."

"Sounds like a good idea," Rob commented.

"Thank you," Linda said with a smile that quickly turned to a frown. "John was expected to carry out the garbage before he went to a friend's house, but he was adamant that he would not. When I told him he was not going to his friend's because of his disrespectful attitude, he yelled 'watch me' and stormed out of the house. I assumed he had gone to his friend's, but when I called there later that afternoon, he had not shown up."

"I know this is difficult," Carrie reached across the table and touched the crying mother's arm, "but do you think John ran away, or do you think someone may have picked him up?"

Linda dabbed the tears, and looked at Carrie with the saddest eyes she had ever seen. "I would hate to think that John is so vindictive that he would put his family through this heartache on purpose. But, then again, he is a headstrong young man. I hate to say this, but I would not be surprised if he is out there somewhere enjoying his life without a care in the world. Excuse me." Linda, unable to keep her composure anymore, half-ran into the house, letting out a heart-breaking sob before the door closed behind her.

Rob and Carrie sat in silence, unable to find the right words to say. It seemed as if every visit to victim's homes was becoming more and more heart-wrenching.

The door opened minutes later, and Anita came out holding a framed picture of John. "Mrs. Linda says she is sorry, but this has become too much for her and she will not be able to answer any more questions. Here is the most recent picture of John. Now, if you will follow me, I will show you out."

Carrie took the framed picture and looked down at a handsome young man with blonde hair and large, deep-green eyes that were almost identical to his mother's. His smile was large and captivating and accented a squared-off jaw.

When they reached the front door, Rob handed Anita a business card and thanked her for her time. The maid smiled and closed the door gently behind them.

"Well, that was fun," Rob said in a tone dripping with sarcasm. He put on his sunglasses and looked around the quiet neighborhood.

They walked to the car and got in. Rob started the ignition and turned on the a/c to high. "I have one question. What makes this a kidnapping?"

"What do you mean?" Carrie asked, wiping a drop of sweat from her brow with the back of her hand.

"The mother mentioned the kid going to the park. He was going to a friend's house, she said. In fact, looking through the file earlier, there was no mention of the park in the police report, other than a slight mention that there was a park across the street from the home."

"Sounds like the police had an unsolved case and lumped it in with the rest of the kidnappings to avoid embarrassment."

"But why? This case barely made the news. Why would the police feel the need to hide this one?"

They both knew there were no immediate answers to the questions, but they were determined to come up with some solutions, even if it killed them.

<u>29</u>

Thomas was the first one to hear the gunshot in the distance. Stephen was following him and was paying more attention to the river than where he was walking when he ran into the back of the scared boy.

"What are you doing?" he asked irritated. His empty stomach was starting to ache, and that was doing wonders for his demeanor.

"Didn't you hear that?"

"Hear what?"

"Gunshot." The word was accented by another gunshot in the distance. It was nowhere close to the boys, but was still a scary sound.

Stephen could feel goose bumps starting to form on his arms. As much as he just wanted to run home and collapse in his mother's arms, be knew he had to be strong, or they would never make it through alive. "We're in the woods, and people hunt in the woods. It's nothing to be afraid of."

"But what if it's him?"

Stephen walked around Thomas and continued his trek down the river. "What if it is? He's nowhere near us. Let's go."

The summer heat was starting to wear on Dane. His body didn't feel right, his hands and feet were still tingling from the hit, and walking around was not helping. He wanted to tell his partner that it was over, the kids were gone, and they should just head back home, but he knew that was not a good idea. He wiped his brow and strained his ears to tune into sounds other than the dead leaves crunching beneath his feet.

Exhaustion was about to take over his body when suddenly his partner stopped and knelt in the thick blanket of leaves and underbrush.

"Water" was the only word spoken.

Dane did not kneel, but rather leaned against a tall pine tree and squinted toward the horizon. Far in the distance he could hear the refreshing sound of running water. "It's the Holston River," Dane said with a slight smile. He grew up in these woods and spent many summer days fishing in the great Holston River. If the kids had made it this far, the river would be a welcome sight.

"Let's head that way," Dane was ordered, and followed willingly. He dare not argue.

30

Carrie and Rob contemplated heading back to the Sheriff's station to drill the sheriff on the Pickering case, but their ride was stopped by the smells of street vendors cooking up southern classics, and the sound of bluegrass music echoing between the big buildings of downtown.

Rob pulled into a pay-to-park lot, handed the man standing at the entrance $20, and pulled into the lot. Without saying a word, they both knew their day was done, and they were going to spend their time enjoying the festivities.

They waded through the throngs of tourists and natives that had flooded the streets, stopping occasionally when their noses drew them to tents where cooks, their faces glistening from the heat, cooked everything from Greek gyros to Italian sausages piled high with greasy onions and peppers. Several vendors sold their wares and Carrie found herself drawn to the turquoise jewelry and handmade quilts that reminded her of the summers she spent helping her grandmother make beautiful quilts that would soon make their way to the beds of her loved ones.

The heat of the day was soon forgotten as they downed ice cream cones and shaved ice. Rob took her hand and led her to the river bank where a local band was playing their versions of popular country songs. They sat near the water and watched the boats float lazily down the Cumberland. The water looked cool and inviting. As relaxing as the day seemed, Carrie still found herself thinking about the missing children.

Rob must have been reading her mind. "So, what's next on the agenda?"

"Well, we still have one more case to investigate, and then ... I don't know."

Rob placed his chin on the top of Carrie's head. "I say we go ahead and get that done; We still have time today. Then we can head back to my place where I will fix a nice dinner and we will forget about this mess until Monday. I am not working on this tomorrow. I don't know about you, but I need a day off."

Carrie smiled and nodded her head. "Agreed."

Landon Rodriguez had a beautiful smile accented by chubby cheeks, and a large cluster of dark, curly hair sitting on top of a round face. His eyes were two large, brown buttons which brought out his tan skin. The picture was obviously a school picture. Carrie held the photo in her hands as Rob drove to a neighborhood just south of downtown. He turned onto a sleepy street in desperate need of repairs. Small houses lined each side of the road, and Latin music could be heard echoing through the trees. Hispanic children played soccer and tag in yards with very little grass, each kick stirring up a cloud of dust.

The rest had done Rob and Carrie good, and they were eager to get the investigation started again.

Rob stopped the car in front of a small, wood-framed house with chipped white paint starting to fall off its exterior walls. Toys and bicycles littered the front yard, and as they walked up to the front door, they were greeted by a toddler in diapers pressing her nose against the torn screen door. A faded pink bow was hanging precariously from her short hair, and an empty baby bottle was gripped by her teeth.

Carrie knocked on the doorframe and was greeted by a slew of Spanish words coming from the back of the house. A young boy maybe four years old at tops ran to the door and smiled. Carrie smiled back and asked, "Es su mama en la casa?" The toddler smiled and waddled to the back of the home. The talking stopped abruptly, and a small, tan face appeared around a wall.

"Hola," Carrie said in an exaggerated voice, "Yo soy Carrie. Habla Ingles?"

A small woman with sad, tired eyes came around the wall wiping her hands on the front of a stained, white, button-up shirt. "Hi, my name is Maria," she responded in perfect English. She came to the screened door, but made no attempt to open it. "How can I help you?"

"We are investigating the disappearance of Landon Rodriguez. Are you a relative of his?"

"Yes, I'm his sister."

"It's a pleasure to meet you. I know you already spoke to the police about Landon, but we are trying to speak with the families and get the whole story."

A look of bewilderment came over the young woman, and her eyes asked the question long before her lips did. "Why?"

"Maria, I am an investigative reporter and I am trying to get all of the information I can. If the police missed anything in this case, I want to find out what they missed and, hopefully, come closer to finding your brother."

Maria unlocked the screen door and opened it. "Come in. Please excuse the mess."

Carrie and Rob stepped into a surprisingly large and immaculate living room. The couch and a recliner were covered with what looked like homemade quilts. A small table/lamp combination sat next to the chair and held a well-read novel, a remote control and a can of soda sitting on a folded napkin. The only item out of place in the room was a plastic dump truck sitting in the middle of the room. The walls were covered with pictures, old and new. A cross hung on the wall over the recliner. The couch sat perfectly in front of a window next to the front door.

They sat down on the couch as instructed and refused drinks from the young lady. She excused herself and returned moments later with the toddler wearing the pink bow under her right arm, and a small boy about six years old holding on to her left hand. Maria sat down on the recliner with the girl in her lap, and the little boy began playing with the toy.

"This is my sister, Lilia, and my brother Luis."

"They are beautiful kids," Rob said genuinely with a smile.

"Thank you. I have another brother, Eddie. He's 16 and isn't home much." Her eyes changed for a moment, and instead of being filled with joy over the compliments about her siblings, she suddenly looked worried, like a mother whose child is late for curfew. She noticed Carrie looking at her and turned away, embarrassed.

"So, tell me about Landon," Carrie asked, looking down at her notebook. She didn't want to frighten the young woman or come off as too intimidating. Just as Maria was about to answer, Rob's cell phone rang, prompting him to excuse himself and answer the call on the front porch.

Maria smiled and looked at Carrie. "Landon is a joy; a sweet boy who always seems to be happy no matter what he is doing. You tell him to go wash the dishes, and he does. Not an argument comes from him. He doesn't need prompting, either. If there is a paper on the floor, he will pick it up. If Lilia needs changing, he changes her. I wish all teenagers were like him."

"Tell me about the day he disappeared."

"You must understand something. My parents, they aren't around too much. My father, he is a truck driver, and he is gone for weeks at a time. He loves us, all of us, and there is always money in the bank for us, but he is never here. When he is, the kids won't leave his side. Mama, the same way. She works two jobs, and when she is home, she is asleep. The kids don't see her much, but when she is sitting here watching TV, they are around her, leaning on her legs, sitting on the arms of the chair."

"So what happened that day?"

"Landon has a friend down the street; her name is Hillary. They have known each other practically since birth. He asked me if he could go down to her house, and I agreed. Why not, you know? About two hours later, Hillary shows up at the door and says she can't find Landon. He is gone. I didn't panic. We walked around the neighborhood looking for him. When it got to be dark, I got worried."

"I can imagine."

"I went out to the street and started calling his name," Maria began ringing her hands, tears made a slow, soft decent down her cheeks. "I called and called, but he never came, so I called the police." Her face changed, from sorrow to anger. Her cheeks grew crimson and her eyes spewed drops of hatred. "Two hours, it took them. Two hours to come to my house and start finding my brother. And when they came here, they were not in a hurry. They didn't care. They jotted down his name, asked for a photo, and left. I don't think they were here for more than 15 minutes."

Carrie could not believe what she was hearing. Was it possible that all those stories of police corruption were true and happening in her backyard? "Maria, I just have a couple more questions." The young girl looked at her and nodded her head. "Did you, or anyone you talked to, remember seeing an older blue car in the area the day Landon disappeared?"

Before Maria could answer, Rob opened the screen door hard, slamming it against the wall and startling the two women. "Carrie, I need to talk to you."

She excused herself and walked out on the porch. "What?"

Rob placed both hands on the wall of the house as if to brace himself. The cell phone in his right hand began ringing, but was ignored. With his head hanging, he said, "They discovered an older model blue car in Knoxville yesterday. There was blood in the back seat, and a body in the front."

Carrie feared the worst. "Oh God, please. Not one of the children. Please." She found herself sobbing uncontrollably, and put her face in her hands. Tears made their way through her fingers and began rolling down her arms. She couldn't explain why the news had struck her so hard.

Rob knelt beside her and tried to comfort her. "It wasn't a child, Carrie. It was an adult male. They are trying to identify him. It wasn't a child."

<u>31</u>

The man saw the scene through his rifle scope, and once he figured out what it was, he ran toward it. It was probably a half mile away.

The sound of the leaves crunching did not bother Stephen anymore. He was weak from hunger and dehydration and his legs were no longer able to support the weight of his body. That happened an hour earlier. He had been lying under a tree watching the clouds pass by through the branches. He could hear the footsteps getting closer and closer, and he didn't care. "Let them kill me," he thought to himself. At least it would be a quick death.

Thomas was not so calm. He heard the footsteps, but terror kept him where he was. He could feel the warmth of his pee as it began to pool under his butt and legs. Normally he would have been embarrassed by this childish act, but not now. He was about to meet the boogeyman.

The hunter stopped when his eyes met the vacant eyes of a child. He laid his rifle down on the wet leaves and walked slowly toward the young face. There was no attempt made by the boy to run. The hunter knelt down and reached out his hand, touching the boy's head gently. "What's your name," he asked softly.

"Stephen."

Movement drew the hunter's attention as Thomas rose, tears streaming down his face in terror. The hunter looked at him with kind eyes. "Don't be afraid, son," he said. "My name is Patrick, and I want to help you and Stephen."

Thomas didn't answer. Patrick leaned over and picked up Stephen. "Come on, boy, he said to Thomas, "and I'll get you all some food and water." He began walking away slowly with Stephen in his arms. Normally Stephen would have fought being carried like a baby, but in that instant, he felt safe.

The haunting sound of footsteps startled E.J., and he balled himself up in as small a space as possible. Ty had told him one time when someone was trying to break into their home to go to the darkest corner of the darkest room and make himself small to hide. E.J. buried his head in his knees and prayed that the boogeyman would leave him alone. He peeked out when he realized that the footsteps were different. The boogeyman walked like a monster, shaking the floor like an earthquake. These steps were different … almost like the sound Ty made when he would come home from work and come into the bedroom to go to sleep.

There was a metal sound on the floor, and then a loud bang, like someone was hitting the wooden door with a log. E.J. could feel the tears welling up in his eyes, and he prayed to God, just like Ty had taught him to. "Whenever you are scared," Ty told him one night, "you close your eyes and you tell God all about it. He will protect you. He will make everything ok, even when it seems like everything is going wrong."

His thoughts were interrupted by the door cracking and flying open, banging on the wall. The room was suddenly filled with light, which blinded E.J. even though his eyes were closed. He didn't look up and prayed to God. The footsteps came closer and then stopped. A hand on his shoulder made him jump and scream. When he opened his eyes in terror, there was a young face and eyes staring at him.

"My name is Landon," the older boy said. "I'm not going to hurt you. I want to help you." He stood up and offered a hand to E.J., who took it timidly and pulled himself off the floor.

32

Though she wanted to find out more about the blue car and who was in it, Carrie struggled to keep her priorities in place. She called *The News* and left a message for Max. She wanted to talk to the lady Mrs. Hoverton had told her about, and then, if she hadn't heard from Max yet, she would go to the newspaper for answers.

The ride to Fullerton was silent. Carrie chose to drive because she knew exactly where she wanted to go, and because she needed to get her thoughts straight.

She parked the car in the same spot she had previously at the park and got out. She pointed out Ty's house, and waved at Mrs. Hoverton, who was once again sitting on the porch drinking lemonade. They then turned and started walking toward a two-story, pink house that faced the park. It was fenced in, and the gate was closed. "Beware of Dog" and several signs indicating the home was protected by several security companies, hung from the fence and littered the yard.

"Overkill," Rob said, pointing to the security signs. "Either this woman is scared of her own shadow, or she has a real fear of her neighbors." Carrie nodded in agreement and walked up to the gate. "Wouldn't you?"

"Go'on in," Mrs. Hoverton yelled from across the park. "She ain't got no dang-old dog in there," she laughed.

Carrie and Rob obeyed and opened the gate. No snarling animals seemed to hear the metal squeaking. They made their way up the cracked sidewalk and knocked on the front door.

"Get the hell off my property 'fore I call the cops," came an angry voice from behind the closed door. Carrie couldn't see anything through the thick film of dirt that covered the windows in front of the home.

"Ma'am, my name in Carrie Stevens, and I …"

"I don't care who you are," interrupted the aging woman, "get off my property."

Rob grabbed Carrie's arm and pulled her back. "Not until you talk to us," he said to Carrie's amazement. He leaned over and whispered, "If we want her out of there, we'll have to lure her. Nothing bothers people like her more than smart-ass young people. Watch, you'll see." He stood upright and crossed his arms across his chest.

It took two minutes for the door to fly open. They expected to see an older woman, but what they got was a tall, young, black man covered in tattoos pointing a gun at them.

<u>33</u>

When Stephen opened his eyes, he thought he was in a dream. He was lying in a large bed in a room with curtains hanging across the windows, and the sweet smell of barbecue hanging in the air. Next to the bed was a small nightstand with a plate of food covered with a napkin and a mason jar with what looked like tea in it, ice cubes floating on the surface.

His stomach told him to eat, but fear encompassed him. What if this was a trap? He saw in a movie one time where the killer made the victim feel safe, so his guard would be down and them BAM! The killer shot the guy in the head. His thoughts were broken by laughter … Thomas' laughter. Stephen sat up in bed and grabbed the plate from the table. Let them kill him; he was hungry.

Stephen was nearly through the plate of barbecue pork, fresh green beans and corn on the cob when he noticed that he was wearing new clothes. The cotton was soft against his skin, and brought an air of comfort over his body. With his stomach full, he climbed out of bed and opened the door to the room. A bright light and the sound of the T.V. made their way down the hallway. Pictures of little kids, and what looked like grandparents hung on both walls down the hallway. He was just about to take his first step when a door opened to his left, and Thomas walked out of the bathroom.

"Stephen!" The boy ran up and gave him a bear hug, which made him feel weird. He pushed the kid off him.

"Where are we?"

"I don't know, but these people are really nice. The old man, his name is Patrick; he's the one who found us. His wife is Luanne, and she cooks … a lot. They have a lot of kids who are grown up, and a lot of grandkids. They remind me of my grandma and grandpa. Come on." Thomas grabbed Stephen's wrist and dragged the youngster down the hall into a large living room.

"Look who's up," Thomas said loudly. Stephen contemplated running back down the hall and into the bedroom, but fought it off. If these people wanted to hurt them, they would have done it by now.

Luann stood up from the couch. She was an older, plump woman with grey hair and a round face. She was wearing a red, plaid button-up shirt and blue jeans. Her chubby fingers held knitting. She smiled a tender smile. "Hello, Stephen. My name is Luann."

Patrick also rose and walked around the back of the couch. He was tall and thin with a full beard and large, bear-like hands. "Welcome to our home, Stephen," he said in a deep, gravelly voice. They both sat down on the couch. Luann continued her knitting and Patrick focused his attention back on the magazine he was reading. Thomas was laying on a large area-rug in the middle of the room playing with a large collection of Matchbox cars, softly making car noises as he moved the metal vehicles in their imaginary world.

Stephen walked to the center of the room and got on the floor with Thomas. He didn't know where he was, or what was going on, but those questions could easily be answered later. For that one instant, he simply wanted to be a kid again.

Dane was the first to notice the shotgun. The steel from the barrel was sticking out from a pile of leaves. He alerted his partner to the discovery.

He stood and looked around. There was not a person in sight. No blood or footprints could be found in the underbrush and leaves. Without saying a word, they both realized that the search for the runaway children ended there. They both turned and trudged back toward the pick-up truck. Dane's head was throbbing, and he was ready to just pack it in and go back home.

He slowed his pace and slung the rifle over his shoulder, rubbing his sweat-covered temples to alleviate the pain. He was not prepared for the blow that sent him to his knees. For a brief moment he looked around, dazed, the vision coming in and out. He fell to his stomach and then rolled over, trying to clear his eyes. His last vision was the barrel of the gun that ended his life.

<u>34</u>

"Whoa," said Rob stumbling backwards as the man with the gun stepped out of the doorway and onto the walkway. "We aren't here looking for any trouble."

"Well trouble just found you, didn't it? My grandma said to get off her property, and unless you want to be hauled out of here in a body bag, then I suggest you turn around and get on out of here."

Heeding the man's advice, Carrie and Rob began walking backwards away from the house.

"Nice plan," Carrie said sarcastically. "Worked out real well, now didn't it?"

"Shut up."

They turned toward the street, only to come face to face with Mrs. Hoverton. "Ricky Plummer, you put that gun away and tell your stubborn grandma to get her lazy butt out here, now." She slowly teetered her way up the walkway and approached the door.

"Grandma said she dint want to see no one," the teen complained. Mrs. Hoverton raised her can and used it to move Ricky out of the way. "Boy, you better get that gun outta my face before I beat you to death. Edna, it's Georgia. Come on out here. These people are trying to find that young boy who's missing." She continued into the house and slammed the door shut. Muffled yelling could be heard coming from inside the home.

Ricky placed the gun in the waistband of his jeans and apologized silently to Carrie and Rob. They accepted and looked at each other, not quite sure what to make out of the whole situation.

Within minutes, Mrs. Hoverton was standing in the door way, motioning for the investigators and Ricky to enter the home.

Carrie was the first to enter, and walked into an immaculate home trimmed with antiques. The couches, tables, and pictures made the room feel like they were living in the Great Depression. Edna was a heavy-set woman with gray hair exploding on top of a worn, chiseled face. She glared at Rob and Carrie before ordering them to sit and telling Ricky to fetch some glasses of tea.

"Well, you wanted to talk to me. Here I am. What do you want?"

Carrie smiled and re-introduced herself. She explained what they were doing, and then asked Edna about the blue car.

"Yeah, I seen it. The guy who was driving it, that reporter, took off out of here like a bat out of hell. That old piece of junk couldn't handle the strain and backfired. Nearly gave me a heart attack."

Carrie suddenly found breathing difficult. "What do you mean 'that reporter?' Who was it? Was it a local man?"

Edna shook her head in agreement and acknowledged the glass of tea being handed to her by Ricky. Carrie and Rob took theirs, too, but didn't drink. "That's my grandson, Ricky. He's a good kid. Had some problems when he was younger, but now he's on the straight and narrow."

Rob smiled at the teen. "Good for you."

Obviously embarrassed, Ricky smiled back and made his way out of the room.

Carrie was just about to begin drilling Edna about the car when her cell phone rang. She excused herself from the room and walked out to the street to take the call.

"Carrie, it's Max. We need to talk."

"I can get over there this afternoon. I'm wrapping up something right now."

"Carrie, I need you to get over here now. It is imperative that I talk to you right now."

"I'm on my way." Carrie ended the call and asked Rob to join her in front of the house. "It was Max," she said to Rob, "I have to go to the newspaper right now. Something is going on."

"I'll come with you ..."

"No," Carrie said sternly. "You need to finish up with Edna. I will call you tonight." She half walked, half ran to the car.

"How am I supposed to get home, Carrie?" Rob called from the porch.

"Call a cab," she said before closing the door and racing down the street. A million thoughts filled her head as she weaved in and out of traffic as she made the quick trip to *The News*.

Carrie pulled into the employee parking lot, ran to the door, and up the stairs to the newsroom. When she opened the glass door leading to the heart of the newspaper, the eerie silence slapped her in the face. No one was talking; in fact, the only noise was the droning emanating from the T.V. in the middle of the room. She could feel eyes on her as she walked to Max's office and knocked on the closed door.

"Come in," came Max's voice from inside. Carrie walked into the room and closed the door behind her. Max was focused on something on his desk, and did not acknowledge her presence, leaving her to stand in an uncomfortable silence for what felt like hours. "Have a seat," he finally said, and Carrie obeyed.

"Carrie, I have some disturbing news to tell you, and it's going to be difficult. I need you to keep it together and process this like a reporter."

"Ok."

"They got a bit of a break in the kidnapping case today. A car that had apparently been spotted at several of the kidnapping areas was located today near Knoxville."

"Yeah," Carrie said, barely able to contain her excitement or keep her butt in the chair, "I told the police about that blue car. It wasn't in any of the reports, but we found out about it from some of the witnesses."

"Good work," Max said, coming around the desk and sitting on the edge in front of Carrie. "What you might not have known is that there was a body found in the car, along with some other items."

"Rob just told me that, but they were still trying to identify the remains."

"Well, they have identified the body, and we are running a story on it tomorrow. I wanted to tell you before you read it. They think they have identified the body, and they think he may be the kidnapper."

"Really! Wow." Carrie jumped up from the seat and stared out the office window, trying to process the information.

"I think you are going to want to sit down," Max said. He walked to the window and stood next to Carrie. "Please, sit down."

She turned at looked at him. If she didn't know better, she would have sworn tears were forming in the gruff editor's eyes. The eyes of the man who was the anchor of the newsroom; who never let a story get to him. The eyes of the man who lost his youngest son to cancer and was back in the newsroom the next day. Suddenly, Carrie was concerned. "Max, just tell me. What is going on?"

"The body in the car … it was Charlie."

The words struck Carrie's knees like a sledge hammer, and before she could catch herself, she was on the floor. She could not control the flood of emotion that seemed to drown her body, and she did not have the strength to fight the sadness that had placed a vice grip on her heart and made breathing a chore. All she could do was lay there shaking her head in disbelief and sob, "no" forcing its way through her lips repeatedly.

For a moment, Charlie was there with her, holding her head, caressing her hair and telling her it was all ok. She saw them walking along the lakeshore talking and laughing. She felt his strong arms around her, holding her tight and whispering softly, "I love you, Carrie," though they both knew it was not romance, just genuine love.

She opened her eyes and realized that Charlie was not there. Max was holding a wet paper towel on her head. "You ok, kid?" he asked with concern.

"It can't be. Not Charlie. He would never hurt a child. Never."

Max didn't say a word. He sat there with her in silence for nearly an hour as she composed herself. Suddenly, she popped her head up, sat up and forced herself to stand up. She had to get out of that suffocating office and go home where she could think seriously and figure it all out.

"Carrie, sit down," Max said softly. "You are in no condition to be driving right now."

Ignoring his plea, Carrie threw open the office door and stormed out of the newsroom. Day had turned to night, and the downtown street festival had become a party. The smell of street food and beer rode on the sounds of live music waltzing its way through the streets. She pulled her keys out of her pocket and forced one between her fisted fingers. The employee parking lot was located beneath a bridge, and walking out there at night had always scared Carrie. She walked with her head down and found herself wiping away tears as she approached her car. She got into the vehicle, locked the door, and laid her head on her arms cradling the steering wheel. "Not Charlie," she repeated over and over.

Was Charlie's car the one Edna saw in Fullerton? If so, what was he doing there, and was his car the one that was seen at the other kidnappings? There had the be an explanation, Carrie insisted. There had to be.

The drive home was one full of pain. Her head swirled with thoughts of Charlie and the brotherly love he had always shared with her, and thoughts of Charlie, the mutilated body found in a car that was connected to the string of kidnappings in the area. Was there really any way he could be connected? Of course not, she thought to herself. But why was he in the car?

She turned into her apartment complex and pulled into the covered parking space. As she walked up the narrow walkway to her house, a slight movement near the base of the bushes next to her door drew her attention. As she got closer, she noticed a small kitten huddled against the bush in fear, a small meow coming from its lips. Carrie picked up the frightened animal and held its trembling body next to hers. Tears made their way down her cheeks, and dropped gently on the kitten.

"I'll call you Charlie."

Rob rang the doorbell nearly two hours after Carrie returned home, and as happy as she was to see him, she was ready to talk just yet. She simply opened the door and walked back into the kitchen without saying a word.

Silently, Rob walked into the living room and sat on the couch, not sure what to say, or even if he should say anything at all. His worries were interrupted by the kitten bouncing its way across the room to attack Rob's shoe string. He gently picked up the ball of fur and held it close, rubbing it's head and back until it curled up in his arms and fell into a purr-filled sleep.

"Should I be jealous?" Carrie asked, standing in the doorway of the kitchen with a glass of soda in each hand.

"I don't know. She's the perfect companion. Doesn't say much, wants constant attention, likes to be held..."

"Yeah," Carrie walked over to the couch and sat slowly next to Rob to keep from startling the kitten, "but there is that whole licking the butt thing. That's kind of a turn off."

Rob chuckled and lay the kitten on the carpet. "True. And I don't think I could handle the fur on the tongue thing either."

Carrie's laughter slowly turned to tears as she laid her head on Rob's shoulder and began to sob. Not knowing what to say, he placed his arm around her and kissed her on the top of her head.

35

T
he man was sitting on the bench at the corner of Orange Ave. and Bartlett St. when the school bus turned onto Bartlett and made its way two blocks to its first stop. The man stood up and followed the bus slowly. About halfway to the stop he reached into his jeans pocket with his gloved right hand, pulled an envelope out, and placed it in the faded blue mail box. Without missing a step, he took off the glove, pulled down his Titans cap, and put on his sunglasses.

Three small children exited the bus. One ran quickly to her mother who was waiting in her car. The other two stopped briefly, confused as to why their nanny, Beatrice, was not waiting for them. After a brief conversation, they decided to wait to see if she showed up, not knowing that she was in their kitchen, and that her life was slowly spilling out onto the just-mopped floor.

The mother in the car was concerned about the children. She glanced at the two innocent faces, but put her worries aside as she listened to her daughter talk excitedly about her day. After buckling the little girl into her car seat, she turned her attention back to the curb where the brother and sister were sitting, and noticed that all that remained was the little boy's backpack, the name "Willie" scrawled across the front in crayon.

The letter arrived at *The News,* Monday morning, and was sitting on Max's desk by noon, along with nine other pieces of mail. Max came into his office at 3, and poured himself a shot of whiskey before finally noticing the envelopes. The first five pieces of mail were junk, and were tossed at the wastebasket and scattered on the floor. The sixth piece was the letter.

Max slid his chubby finger under the flap, and tore open the envelope. A single sheet of folded paper was inside, and the words on it caused Max to drop the letter and pick up the phone. Within minutes, the Publisher, several editors, and a reporter were standing in the small office waiting to find out what was going on.

Reporter Deb Horace closed the office door, and the room went silent.

"A letter came today," Max began, wiping the beads of sweat off his brow with the sleeve of his shirt, "and it was … disturbing. The police have been called. Before I get into the contents of this letter, what is said in this meeting and in this office needs to remain behind closed doors. If I find out there have been any leaks, everyone in here will be fired. Am I clear?"

Everyone, including the Publisher, Zachary Garvin, nodded their heads.

"Good." Max picked up the paper and held it in the air. "I'm not going to read this to you, because most of it is not relevant; however, it is the last paragraph that is disturbing. Basically, it is a threat on the kidnapped children. According to the sick son of a bitch who wrote this, he wants money … a lot of it. If he doesn't get it tonight, he is going to kill one child per hour until he does. He also claims to have captured to more children, and that the 'hammer will fall' tonight."

The silence was suffocating, and no one knew what to say. "What is the plan," Deb finally said, echoing the exact thoughts of everyone in the room.

"We need to find out if any children have been reported missing over the last day or two, and then we wait for the police," Max answered.

"I'm on it," Deb said, and left the room.

Within minutes the office was empty. For the first time in his professional career, Max felt overwhelmed.

<u>36</u>

Carrie awoke refreshed Tuesday morning with the kitten purring gently next to her. The aroma of coffee filled the air, and she was glad that she remembered to set the timer. She loved that time of the morning, when she could just lie in her bed in silence and wake slowly, the birds chirping a happy song outside her bedroom window. The peacefulness was interrupted by the phone ringing, and Rob ordering her to the newspaper before hanging up.

She didn't take the time to shower and quickly dressed in a pair of faded jeans and a yellow t-shirt. She pulled her hair into a sloppy ponytail and ran out of the apartment.

If she had taken the time to turn on the radio during her long drive to *The News*, she would have been better prepared for what she was about to encounter; but haste and worry took off her normal routine, and before she knew it, she was pulling into the parking lot. News trucks lined the street in front of the newspaper building. They must have found out about Charlie.

Before she was completely out of her car, Rob ran over, took her hand, and led her to the employee entrance. He flashed a card to the security guard, and practically dragged her to the newsroom. Dozens of broadcast media members were there with their cameras and microphones. A makeshift stage had been set up in the back of the newsroom, and all eyes were on the podium and microphones sitting near the wall.

Carrie and Rob shoved their way to an adjacent wall and waited for the conference to start. Confusion quieted the questions filling Carrie's mind, and she instinctively grabbed a reporter's notebook from her back pocket and a pencil to take notes.

The room suddenly fell into silence as Max, Sheriff Tate, Harlan Stanton, and Councilman Billy Tyler made their way to the podium area. Sheriff Tate stepped up to the podium.

"Ladies and gentlemen, we're here to update you on some recent events that have come to our attention. We will all say what we have to say, and there will not be a question and answer." He glanced quickly towards Harlan, who looked disappointed, and cleared his throat. "Yesterday afternoon, the Nashville Sheriff's Office was contacted by *Nashville News* Editor Max Worth concerning a letter that he received. The letter contained information about the recent rash of kidnappings in the area, and some other information that I cannot discuss right now.

"Approximately two hours after receiving Mr. Worth's phone call, another call came to the Sheriff's Department. Nashville Councilman William Tyler called to report that his two children, William Jr., eight years old, and Miranda, six years old, were last seen exiting their school bus yesterday afternoon. He also called to report an apparent homicide at his home. The name of the adult victim has not been released.

"The Nashville Sheriff's Department is working hard to end this string of kidnappings and to apprehend those responsible. We will not stop until each of the missing children is home safe with their families. Thank you."

Billy was the next to speak. His eyes, red from what had to have been hours of stress and tears, looked worn. "My name is Councilman William Tyler, and I would like to take this opportunity to beg the person or persons who have my children to please keep them safe from harm. Miranda and Willie have been through so much already in their young lives. They never had the opportunity to know their mother, and you have taken them from the only person they have left in the world. I implore you … please take care of them and return them to the safety and security of their home." Billy became overwhelmed by grief and laid his head on the podium. His sobs were deafening, and his tears seemed to spread to nearly everyone in the room. Carrie saw Rob wipe his eyes, and noticed that even Harlan was crying.

Max put his arm around Billy and led him from the podium and away from the throng of cameras. Harlan took the opportunity to make his way to the podium, and Carrie wondered if his tears were merely crocodile tears meant solely for the press.

"My name is Harlan Stanton, and I am lead councilman for the Nashville City Council. I would like to let the community and Mr. Tyler know that we are in complete support of the investigation of these tragic, tragic, kidnappings, and we will do whatever possible to aid in the recovery of these children."

Carrie had heard enough. She pushed her way through the crowd and toward her car. Rob followed. When she reached the car, she hit the roof as hard as she could with both fists; tears of rage forced their way through her clinched eyes and burned a trail down her cheeks. She struggled to keep from pounding her head into the door frame. Enough is enough, she whispered to herself. When is it all going to end?

Rob came up behind her and placed his hand gently around her shoulder. Normally, she would have collapsed as a sobbing child in his arms, but not that day. She was mad. Billy's tormented face kept showing up in her mind, making her determination grow stronger by the minute.

She quickly swiped the tears from her eyes and face with clinched fists and turned toward Rob with a motion so sudden, it nearly knocked him off his feet. "What now," she asked.

"We need to get a copy of that letter ... the one sent to Max. We need to see what it says, see if it offers any clues, and go from there."

"I'll get a copy."

<u>37</u>

No matter how nice the house was or how good the food tasted, Stephen was ready to go home. The first time he mentioned it, which was during dinner a couple of days ago, his inquiry was ignored. Luanne and Patrick were nice enough, and they doted on the boys like grandparents, but they weren't Stephen's parents, and he just wanted to go home.

Stephen was lying in bed trying to think of ways he could bring up the topic again when Patrick knocked and opened the door.

"Hey, buddy. I'm heading into town to get some food and stuff. Is there anything you would like?"

A flashbulb exploded over Stephen's head, and he shot up. "Can I go with you?"

Patrick paused before agreeing. "Boat leaves in 10 minutes," he said cheerfully before closing the door.

Stephen jumped out of bed and quickly put on his coat and shoes. He formed a plan in his mind, and needed to tell Thomas before they left.

Walking quietly down the long hallway, he slowly opened the door to Thomas's room and peeked inside. The boy was lying on his stomach on the much-too-large bed, engulfed in a quilt and reading a book. Stephen walked quietly over and sat down on the bed.

"Get dressed. We're getting outta here."

Thomas turned and looked through weary eyes. It was the first time Stephen was able to look at him and see something other than a scared little kid with tears running down his cheeks. In that moment, he looked comfortable, without a care in the world, like most boys his age should be. His hair was clean, his clothes washed. "I don't wanna go."

"Patrick's leaving here in 10 minutes to go into town. I'm going with him, and then I am going home. Don't you miss your family and friends?"

Thomas seemed to think about the question for a moment, and then answered with a resounding "No."

Stephen was stunned by the response. How could he not miss his family? Stephen longed for the day he could play with his best friend in the park, just a couple of kids without a care in the world. What was wrong with this boy? "Well, I'm leaving. I want to go home." He rose off the bed and started walking toward the bedroom door.

"Stephen," came Thomas's soft voice from the bed.

Stephen turned and looked at the innocent face.

"Thank you," Thomas said before turning back to his book. It was the last time the boys would see each other again.

Patrick and Stephen rode in silence down the winding road that finally ended in the middle of a small town. The truck stopped at blinking red light. The two lane street in front of them looked like a stereotypical small town painting. Cars were parallel parked on both sides of the street, and the sidewalks were crowded with people taking advantage of the cool air nighttime brought.

Patrick turned left on the street labeled "Main" and drove about two blocks before pulling into a parking lot littered with rusty, dented metal shopping carts. Smith's Grocery sat at the end of the lot, and looked as run down as its carts. Patrick pulled into a parking space near the store's entrance, and waited for Stephen to catch up. He grabbed a cart with a wobbly wheel and loudly made his way into the store with Stephen by his side.

Shopping was a slow, drawn-out practice for Patrick. He made it a point to look at the label of every item he picked up off the shelf before placing it back on the shelf or in the cart. This routine worked to Stephen's advantage. As Patrick turned at the end of one aisle on his way to the next, Stephen ran as fast as he could toward the front of the store. He sped past curious shoppers and suspicious cashiers, rammed himself through the front door and stopped at the street. He looked desperately up and down the road hoping for some sign of a police officer, and breathed a sigh of relief when he saw a uniformed man walk out of a store carrying an ice cream cone.

Ignoring Patrick's loud orders for him to return to the store, Stephen ran down the sidewalk, weaving in and out of passersby until he reached the sheriff's deputy. The officer stopped mid lick and looked at the out of breath youngster next to him.

"Can I help you, son?"

Working desperately to get the air flowing in and out of his tired lungs, Stephen bent over and struggled to catch his breath. "My name is Stephen Bascombe, and I want to go home." A tear slipped from his right eye, and he realized that it was the first time he had cried since the whole ordeal had begun.

Carrie felt like a failure as she made her way back into the building that housed *The News*. She wanted this to be her big break, but the way things seemed to be going, that was not going to happen.

The throngs of news trucks that had once lined the street in front of the newspaper had thinned out as anxious reporters made their way back to their various newsrooms and prepared to inform the world of this breaking story. Unlike her excited journalist friends, Carrie walked slowly up the steps, head hanging low. She wasn't quite sure why she felt like such a failure, but the feeling was definitely there, and it was overwhelming.

Once she reached the glass doors that led into the newsroom, she tried in vain to straighten her hair before entering. The chatter of voices that filled the room earlier was replaced with the click-clack of fingers on computer keyboards.

Carrie reached Max's office, and noticed that his door was closed. She knocked quietly, half hoping he was not there or was in an important meeting.

"Come in," came a tired voice from behind the dark-wood door.

"Hey Max, it's me," Carrie said gently, peering around the door.

Max was sitting at his desk, his head buried in his hands. His tie was loosened, and the top two buttons were undone. He looked up at Carrie with sad, red eyes. "What's up?"

Carrie sat down on the edge of one of the chairs in front of his desk, and leaned forward. "Are you OK?"

"I'm exhausted." Max sat back in his chair and began rubbing his face like doing so would erase the stress that was leaving deep scars in his forehead. "You wait all your life for that one big story, you know? And you have already planned how you will approach that story – the type of questions you would ask, how to deal with the emotion. Then something like this happens, and your excitement is replaced with a feeling of helplessness."

"You always said I could let the emotion affect the journalism. Same goes for you, Max."

He looked up at the ceiling in search of an answer. "And I meant that, Carrie," Max finally offered softly. "I thought after September 11 that no story would ever have that kind of emotional impact on me.

When I saw those planes slam into the buildings, I fought hard to fight back the tears. And I did." He leaned forward, his face quickly going from hurt to stern. "I walked out into that newsroom, and I was their leader. I was stern; strong. And when it became too much, I was able to fight the emotion and power through."

"So what is the difference now, Max. Find that inner strength again."

"The difference is that I didn't know anyone in the twin towers. My children were in preschool with Billy's kids. My daughter Maddie played soccer with Miranda. How do I explain this to Maddie?"

Carrie was at a loss for words. Though she was not a parent herself, she knew all too well the horror a parent must face in difficult situations. She knew, because she had been the recipient of bad news at a young age.

It had been an unusually cold November morning. It was Thanksgiving, and if she thought long and hard enough, she could still smell the Turkey baking in the oven. Her father, the Sheriff in a neighboring community, had been called to work that morning. He never came home again.

Carrie remembered all too well her mother sitting her down on the sofa and explaining how sometimes God needed Daddies to come to heaven and help Him, and how she understood it was hard for Carrie, but she would just have to accept it. She fought hard, even at the age of eight, that she should not cry and she struggled to keep her emotions in her throat, just as her mother was doing, until her mother left. Once the door shut, Carrie screamed and cried into her pillow, and she never cried about it again.

Max was just going to have to be that strong figure for Maddie, and as much as he would want to just break down and sob, he couldn't. Carrie wanted to tell him that, but she couldn't. She simply patted his arm, promised to be there if he wanted to talk, and left the office.

Once she reached her car, she was that frightened 8-year-old girl who just found out her father was gone. She sat her right arm across the top of the steering wheel, placed her head on her arm and cried.

38

Surprisingly, the children remained quiet during the trip to the cabin. They had not said a word except for the little girl who asked if she could go to the restroom. He was ready to threaten their lives if they got out of hand, but so far, that was not needed. In fact, he even bought them candy and soda at the gas station, and was pleasantly surprised to see them both buckled in the back seat of the sedan when he returned with the goodies.

The dirt road leading up to the cabin had not taken recent rains well, and had become more of a path than a road. The car slid and struggled to keep traction, and he could feel his knuckles turning white as he worked to keep the car from sliding down the edge of the mountain.

The sun was slowly dropping below the horizon, leaving a trail of orange in the sky. He smiled when he saw smoke from the cabin and pulled the car in next to the pick-up truck.

The children unbuckled their seatbelts and waited for the man to open the door. Two sets of curious eyes greeted him as he opened the back door of the car and led the youngsters into the cabin. He was not prepared for what he saw inside.

She was sitting on the couch staring at the fire. Her plaid shirt was filthy, as were her jeans. Mud-caked boots sat next to the door.

"What's going on," he asked.

She looked at him with pleading, bloodshot eyes. She reached out her hand which held a bottle of liquor. "They're all gone," she slurred. "All of 'em … gone."

He took the children back to the room where E.J. should have been, and locked the door behind him. Once he re-entered the living room, he took the bottle from her and threw it against the wall over the fireplace. The smell of alcohol filled the room. "What do you mean, they're gone? Where the hell are they?"

"I don't know. I just don't know. Dane said two of 'em had disappeared, and we went out to track them. We never found 'em."

He rubbed his forehead in disbelief, and growled, "Where's Dane?"

Something about the question sent the drunk woman into a fit of laughter. She fell back on the couch and regained what composure she could. "He's dead; dead as a doornail. He's out there in them woods somewheres and I hope some bear or deer has found his worthless ass and his having a nice dinner."

Before he could control himself, he grabbed her by the front of her shirt and pulled her off the couch. Her eyes grew to the size of quarters as he lifted her, her feet dangling beneath her. "What happened to Dane, you psychotic bitch?"

"I shot him. Killed him. He let them get away."

He dropped her to the floor, spun around and began punching the wall. He hit is as hard as he could until his knuckles were raw and bleeding. When the anger subsided, the pain took over, and he backed up and sat on the couch holding his injured hand.

She sat there for a minute before standing and facing him. "I never wanted this. I never wanted to be here, and you knew that from the beginning. You left us out here in the middle of nowhere to fend for ourselves. What did you think was going to happen? Dane was my friend."

It was his turn to laugh. "Your friend? You killed him. You shot and killed him and talked about his body being used as food, and now you are telling me he was your friend?"

"You left us out here, dared us to play this game, threatened us if we didn't, and expected us to keep our sanity?" The alcohol was slowly starting to wear off. Her eyes were angry. "He messed up the game. He broke the rules, and they got away. What the hell was I supposed to do? Someone had to pay a penalty for the mistake. Dane paid it with his life."

With that, she grabbed a jacket off the coat rack near the door and stormed out. He expected to hear the rumble of the pick-up truck's engine, but silence filled the room.

He walked to the door and opened it. She was sitting on the edge of the porch smoking a cigarette. He sat down next to her and took a cigarette from the package she offered.

"I can't take anymore," she finally said between puffs. "I'm done. I just want to be done."

Without looking at her, he said, "So, let's end it."

"How?"

"Let's take the kids somewhere and drop them off. Be done with this whole mess."

She looked at him with hope. "Are you serious?"

"Yep. All the money in the world isn't worth this. These kids ... let's do this. Let's drop them off somewhere and move on. We don't even have to stay here. We'll leave the state. Clean slate."

She jumped off the porch and hugged him tight. He ran his thin hands across her back and kissed her gently on the neck. "Let's go."

Stephen had told the story at least seven times and was tiring. He had watched enough cop shows to know that they didn't believe him and were trying to find some sort of discrepancy between the stories ... but there were none.

They had been nice enough, though. They offered him a cheeseburger and fries for dinner, and his request for a chocolate shake had been met within minutes. He didn't particularly like sitting alone in the mirrored room for so long, but he was sure they were calling his parents or something. He was confident that the next person who opened the door would be his mother or father.

Within an hour, the door opened, but it wasn't a parent who opened it. It was a tall, slender man in a sheriff's uniform. He closed the door gently behind him and walked to a chair across the table from Stephen. The boy loved the way the leather gun belt squeaked with every move the man made and how he had to walk with his arms stuck out a bit from his side because of the handgun on his right hip, and the walkie-talkie on his left hip.

"Hi there, Stephen. My name is Sheriff Marvin Mater." His smile was broad and showed nearly all of his teeth. He had a thick moustache that completely covered his top lip and it was sprinkled with gray whiskers. He reached out his hand and Stephen shook at as he was taught to do as a display of good manners. "So, I here you ran into a bit of trouble?"

"Yes, sir. I was taken from the park near my home by this guy. Me and my friend, Thomas, broke out of the house we were being held in and here I am."

The sheriff leaned back in his seat. "Ahh, I see. And where is this friend of yours ... Thomas. Why isn't he here?"

"Well, when we were in the woods, this man, Patrick, found us and took us to his home. Thomas likes it there, but I miss my mom and dad. I want to go home. Just call them. You won't even have to take me there. They'll come and get me."

"Now, now, Stephen. Just calm down a minute or two. We talked with Patrick. Do you know who he is?"

Stephen was confused. "What do you mean?"

The sheriff smiled again and rose from his chair. He walked over to one of the mirrored walls and began straightening his moustache. "Patrick, or Mr. Youngblood, as we like to call him, is the pastor here at the Millersville Baptist Church. He's a well-respected man in our community. I told him your account of what happened, and he agreed. All expect for the part about Thomas. See, Mr. Youngblood said he only found you out there in the woods, alone."

Stephen could feel the anger rising from the pit of his stomach. "He's lying. Thomas is at his house, I swear it." He had a death grip on the arms of the chair, and was pushing so hard against the table with his chest that he could feel a bruise forming.

The sheriff smiled a smile that made Stephen want to jump across the table and punch him. Instead, he sat back in the chair and looked at his hands which were now folded in his lap. He had said enough, and it was time for him to shut up. If they weren't going to believe him, he wasn't going to try and convince them anymore.

Sheriff Tate was sitting at his desk working on his fourth hour of paperwork when the phone rang. Normally he would have cursed the phone for interrupting him and then his secretary for letting the call through, but on that day, he needed a break from writing.

"Tate," he answered while sitting back in his chair and throwing his feet on the desk.

"Sheriff Tate, this is Sheriff Marvin Mader from Cumberland County."

"Good afternoon, sheriff. What can I do for you today?"

"Well, Tate, seems I may have a refugee from your fine city. We have a young man here named Stephen Bascombe who claims he was taken from Nashville and somehow wound up in Millersville."

Sheriff Tate shot out of his seat as if someone and laid a hot branding iron under him. The toothpick he had been chewing on since that morning fell out as his mouth dropped open in amazement. Was this possible? "Yes sir, Mr. Mater, we've been looking for this youngster for quite a while. I'd like to talk to him. I am on my way."

Tate picked up the phone again and made a series of phone calls in order to locate various files, and notify people important to the case. The one person he did not, and would not, contact was Harlan. The councilman had a way of finding information on his own, and the sheriff was confident that Harlan would hear the news before Tate even left the city.

The sheriff gathered up all the files and headed down to his SUV where Detective Yanni Plower was waiting for him. The two made their way onto the interstate and headed west for the two-hour drive to Millersville.

39

Carrie pulled her car into the parking garage and found a space near the front. She freshened up her makeup and headed for Rob's apartment, which was two blocks down Broadway. The sidewalks were busy, but not overwhelming, which allowed Carrie the time to think about the case instead of worrying about weaving in and out of tourists.

Once she reached his building, she climbed the old, creaky stairs and knocked on his apartment door. The old man who was sitting under the window at the end of the hall the first time she went to Rob's apartment was gone … an empty, dusty whiskey bottle now sat where the man once did.

Rob opened the door and made Carrie's heart flutter for a moment. He stood in front of her in a pair of gym shorts with no shirt. He was rubbing his hair with a blue-striped towel as drops of water made their way down his chiseled chest and abs. He smiled at her and stepped back to let her in.

The apartment was much cleaner than the last time she had visited; Carrie noticed that the old, worn-out couch with the missing leg had been replaced by a newer, but obviously used sofa. The TV was on and a video game was paused on the screen.

"Have a seat. I just got out of the shower."

She fought the desire to respond with sarcasm, and nodded. "Take your time." What she really wanted to do was offer to help him. Carrie chuckled at her cattiness and sat on the sofa.

She was not there for a minute when her cell phone began ringing. A quick glance at the screen indicated it was Harlan. She contemplated just ignoring the call, but something inside told her it was important.

"Hi Harlan," she offered cheerfully.

"I need you and Rob to get to my office now. Something has come up and you all need to get on it."

"What's going on?"

"Get here, now. I'll be expecting you in 10 minutes." Harlan's voice was hurried and harsh.

Carrie closed her phone. "Rob, Harlan just called. We gotta get going."

He appeared in the bedroom doorway, dressed in a pair of faded jeans and a blue t-shirt. Shaving cream covered the lower part of his face. "What's up?"

"I wish I knew. He wants us there in 10 minutes."

Rob nodded that he had heard her, and headed back into the bedroom. Carrie couldn't help but fear what lie ahead. Hopefully it wasn't another missing child. Hopefully a child's body hadn't been found. She didn't know much, but what she did know was that the news couldn't be good.

Carrie hated the smell of Harlan's office suite. The odor reminded her of her brother's room when her mother would cover up the smell of his old tennis shoes with a few quick sprays of Lysol. They had been instructed to sit and wait by the office secretary, and had been sitting for 20 minutes before they were allowed to go back to his office.

As was the case the first time they met, Harlan was on the phone. Carrie and Rob slipped quietly into the two chairs in front of his massive desk and waited, trying to make out what was being said in the quiet phone conversation.

Harlan finally placed the phone down gently on his desk. "We've had a bit of news today. One of the missing boys turned up in Millersville near the North Carolina border. Sheriff Tate is on his way there, and I want you two there as well."

"With all due respect, Harlan, I don't think the sheriff is going to want a couple of civilians there trying to put in on his work."

Harlan's face grew crimson as he clasped his hands together and interlocked his fingers. "I don't give a damn what Tate wants. I want you two out there. You have a big story to write, and there are still other kids missing, and I want you two slap dab in the middle of this. Am I making myself clear?"

Carrie was about to speak again when she felt Rob grab her hand. "Yes, sir, I think we got it," he said while gently squeezing her hand. It was his way of telling her to shut up, and she complied.

"Good. Get out of here, and I expect daily updates on what is going on out there," Harlan said with a smug grin and a quick glare at Carrie.

She pushed her chair back hard and stormed out of the office, fighting to keep the streams of anger from rolling down her cheeks.

Once she reached the sidewalk in front of the building, she closed her eyes and let her face soak up the sun's rays. Carrie stood there until Rob came out and put his arm around her shoulder.

"We need to get some clothes together and…," Rob began before he was interrupted.

"No! I'm done. I want this over with. I'm tired of the emotions. I'm tired of the worry. Count me out." She broke free of his gentle hands and began walking briskly down the street.

She looked down at her hands and her nail covered with peeling flecks of nail polish and felt tears welling up again. Since this whole mess started, her life had become one crying spell after another, and she was tired of it. Never before had she been like this. This was not her. She was never that weepy girl who toyed with people's emotions to get their attention. She never walked away from a fight, but all she could think about was going home.

Carrie could hear Rob calling her name, but judging by the distance, he obviously was not following her. Good, she thought, because just the thought of Rob being angry or upset with her was more than she could handle.

Before she knew it she was jogging down the street, weaving in and out of the throngs of people window shopping and the homeless people with their hands out looking for spare change.

Once she reached her car, she started the engine and got on the interstate heading south, just like her life seemed to be going.

When Landon and E.J. heard the sound of a vehicle coming up the mountain, they quickly grabbed what they were eating and headed out the back door. E.J. thought they were going to the small shed on the right of the cabin and started running in that direction until Landon stopped him and pulled him back. "You don't want to go there," he said to the boy, and held his hand as they made their way to the woods.

They found some thick underbrush that provided enough cover to hide, yet still allowed them to see the cabin. Within minutes they heard yelling from inside the structure and then the front door of the cabin open and slam closed. Landon began crawling slowly on his stomach around the cabin, remaining in the cover of the trees, and noticed two people on the porch. Their voices were muffled, but the angry words seemed to be over.

The two boys quietly ate their food and waited for the strangers to either go to bed or leave, their hands shaking with every movement.

40

Whoever had leaked the story was going to be fired, Tate thought as he pulled into the town of Millersville and saw the gaggle of media trucks nearly blocking the road. A line of reporters with cameras facing them snaked their way down the sidewalk and filled the grocery store parking lot.

Tate pulled his SUV around the back of the two-story brick building that housed the sheriff's office and slipped through the back door with Det. Yanni Plower close behind them. They climbed the stairs to the second floor and walked to the front of the building. A small wooden desk in the front of the door served as an information center and a sleepy-eyed officer sat behind it reading a new edition of "Field and Stream." Behind him was the main patrol room which was tiny compared to what Tate was used to. The entire room held three desks and two closed-door interrogation rooms in the back.

"Sheriff Tate here to see Sheriff Marvin Mader please."

The young deputy nodded his head toward the back of the room. "He's meetin' with the media right now. You can go sit in his office if ya want to. It's the one in the corner," he said without even raising his head.

Tate fought the urge to snatch the magazine away from the kid and teach him some manners, and quickly walked to the back of the room.

Mader's office was tiny and cramped. A small desk, office chair and two folding chairs took up the majority of the room. A filing cabinet sat in one corner, and it was covered with files and papers that were also cascading down the side of the cabinet and onto the floor. A bookcase sat near the office door, and the thick gathering of dust let Tate know that nothing on that bookcase had been touched or moved in years.

"Nice place," Plower said in a voice oozing with sarcasm.

"You gotta start somewhere. My first job was in a one-horse town in Ohio. Sometimes the boredom of a place drives you harder to be a better officer because you want to get out there in the mix of things quicker."

Plower was a veteran on the force and had lost his drive years ago. Nearing 60, he was close enough to retirement age to have become a bitter man, and he was counting the days until he could collect his pension and retire somewhere in Florida.

Despite his sour disposition, and his entire wardrobe that seemed to contain nothing but black suits, white shirts, and striped ties, Plower was still the best detective on the force, and Tate was glad to have him on this case.

Neither of the men were prepared for what walked through the door. To say that Sheriff Mader looked like Andy Griffith's identical twin would be a severe understatement. From his wavy, dark hair, to his plain brown uniform, to his shined black boots, Tate halfway expected whistling to start penetrating the air at any point.

Mader sat down behind his desk and smiled. "Good afternoon, gentlemen, and welcome to Millersville."

"Good afternoon, Sheriff. This is Yanni Plower, one of the detectives on the case." Plower reached across the desk and shook hands with Mader, who then opened a desk drawer and pulled out a pack of cigarettes. He quietly opened the pack, pulled one out, and lit it, immediately filling the small office with smoke.

Tate could feel the anger creeping up his neck, turning his ears hot. He coughed and asked "When can we see the youngster?"

Mader smiled and placed the cigarette on the edge of his desk with the burnt end hanging over the floor. "Well, I think we have some paperwork to fill out, and some talking to do, so I suggest you just go ahead and book you a room at the Millersville Inn, just down the road apiece, and hopefully we can get you three together tomorrow afternoon, if we're lucky."

Tate could see the smug grin make its way across Mader's face, and he knew the small-town Sheriff was thoroughly enjoying his power over the big-city cops. As much as he wanted to argue, he simply stood up and tipped his hat. "That will be fine, Sheriff." He pulled a card out of his front shirt pocket and handed it to Mader. "Here is my card ... my cell phone number is on the back. You just let me know when you are ready."

Tate turned and walked out of the office with Plower following, mumbling under his breath the entire time.

Carrie reached the Alabama line in an hour, which was a record for her. She exited off the interstate and began the scenic drive to her hometown of Hytop, population 311. The air was different down there, Carrie would always say. Time moved slower, and so did the people. There was no rush, no deadlines. Just a group of southern people who knew the ins and outs of each other's lives, and would always offer a helping hand if needed.

Carrie turned onto Hytop Road and was home. It wasn't really a town to speak of … Mobile homes dotted the landscape. The Food Stop was the biggest business in town, and on Friday and Saturday nights, all of the local teenagers would flood the parking lot in their pick-up trucks and blare music. The fire department was volunteer, and the police force was non-existent. In her 22 years of life, Carrie had never heard of a crime happening in the town except for the occasional kid shoplifting candy.

Just before Hytop Road ended, Carrie turned right onto a dusty, red-clay driveway and through a thicket of trees that opened to a cleared out piece of land that housed a double-wide trailer. She pulled the car next to the broken-down Mustang sitting on the side of the home, and got out. A hot, July afternoon in Nashville could not hold a stick to the dry, suffocating heat of Alabama.

Carrie stepped out of the car and made her way to the front door, which flew open just as she was about to reach out for the door handle; In the doorway stood a tall, shirtless, thin man. He wore a scruffy, spotty beard that accented his gaunt cheeks, and he was covered from head to toe in various types of dirt and grime. His hair, which was in desperate need of a cut, touched his shoulder.

"What the hell do you want," he growled at Carrie.

"Move," she responded, walking up the steps, and shoving the man out of her way as she headed for the living room. "Where's mom?"

"She's working," he said as he brushed by her and flopped down on the worn couch. The trailer shook with the thud.

"Why aren't you working," she inquired before clearing off the love seat and sitting as well. The living room was tinier than she'd remembered. The faux wood paneling was barely visible beneath the tons of framed photos, posters, and a large rebel flag that took up almost an entire wall by itself.

A small television covered in beer cans and dusty DVD cases had the man's full attention as he nursed a beer and half sat, half laid on the couch.

"I asked why you aren't working."

"What the hell do you care? You got your new life up there in Nashville. Don't be worrying about me."

"Look, Jake, it's not fair that mom's out there busting ass while her lazy, 24-year-old son lies around doing nothing all day."

"You ain't here, so you don't need to be running your mouth." Jake stood quickly and adjusted the waistband of his too-big jeans. He stomped into the kitchen and threw open the refrigerator door, causing a jar of pickles to shatter on the floor. A chain of profanities came out of him mouth as he began cleaning up the mess.

Carrie walked across the living room and stood at the entrance of the tiny kitchen. There was not enough room for both of them. Jake was on his hands and knees wiping up the pickle juice and sending clouds of vinegary odor throughout the house.

"Why's it gotta be like this, Jake? Can't we, for once, say hello and enjoy each other's company without World War Three breaking out? I haven't been here in months. Let's catch up."

Jake threw the soaked wad of paper towels on the floor and shot to his feet. "That's right," he yelled, "you ain't been here for months. You ain't called in months, either. We could have all been killed in a fire for all you knew. You think I'm being hard on Mom? How the hell you think you are makin' her feel when she doesn't hear from you?"

"Jake…"

"Do me a favor and get the hell out of here? Just climb back in you your nice, brand-new car, and drive back up to the city where you belong." He shoved her to the side, stormed across the trailer and slammed the door to his room. She contemplated trying to talk to him again, but decided against it when the music began blaring from behind the closed door.

Carrie's mother, Debra, worked in the cafeteria of the high school in Skyline, a small town just south of Hytop. It was time for her to be getting home from work, so Carrie decided to stay in the trailer and wait. It wasn't too long before she heard the sound of gravel crunching on the driveway and the slamming of a car door.

The front door opened, and her mother walked in, still wearing her sunglasses. When she saw Carrie, she dropped her purse on the floor and rushed to hug her daughter. After a long embrace, she held Carrie's face in her hands for a moment and hugged her again.

"Baby, I've missed you," she sobbed in Carrie's ear.

"I've missed you too, mama." Carrie could not help but cry, too. When she left Alabama, she did so with pride holding her head high, and a need for independence that drove her to success. She had convinced herself that she was going to do great things, and that meant getting away from that small-town life.

Being in her mother's arms again made her feel like a child, and for once in a long, long time, she liked being mothered.

When the embrace finally ended, the two women walked into the living room and sat on the couch. They spent what seemed like hours catching up with each other's lives, though Carrie left out the part about her losing her job and the kidnappings.

They laughed and cried, and rebuilt that bond that had been lost the day Carrie walked out the door and made her way to Nashville.

Then there was Jake. "He sure didn't seem to like seeing me again," Carrie said softly.

Debra touched Carrie's hand and shook her head. "Jake's had his problems. You know he's got his Daddy's temper, and my stubbornness. He was working up at the sawmill for a while, but the economy took that opportunity away."

"So he just sits around the house and drinks beer all day? The least he could do is take a shower or something. He looks homeless."

"Oh, him and Bobby Ray have probably been working on that old car all day. He's gotta do something to keep occupied."

Carrie was about to respond when her cell phone rang. Rob. She excused herself and stepped out of the mobile home.

<u>41</u>

E.J. had fallen asleep in the underbrush and was snoring softly. Landon had also fallen asleep, but was awakened by the sound of the front door slamming and the two people walking toward the pickup truck. They threw several duffle bags in the bed of the vehicle, started the loud, sputtering engine, and sped away down the mountain.

Landon woke the younger boy up, and they walked quietly to the front porch. Though they both knew no one remained in the cabin, they weren't taking any chances. A quick look through each of the front windows confirmed that the place was empty.

"I don't think they will be coming back," Landon said confidently. He walked into the kitchen and began scrounging for something to eat.

E.J. flopped down on the couch for a moment, but his anxiousness would not allow him to remain still. He began walking around the room, looking at every item with childlike wonder. He questioned silently where the animal heads on the wall came from, if there were any secret passages behind the bookshelves, and where all of the cool little trinkets that lined all available open space in the room came from. Though the house was not much bigger than his home, it felt like a mansion.

Ty would love this place, E.J. thought. He'd love the coolness in the air and the woods with the thick trees that seemed to hold a thousand secrets in their thick branches. He would love being able to live here without a worry in the world and without having to answer to anyone. Suddenly, E.J. was sad; the tears welled up in his eyes as he thought about his brother and how much he missed him.

"Landon, I want to go home."

Tate kicked his boots off and plopped down on the hard motel bed. The comforter reeked of smoke and previous visitors to the room, and if he thought about how many people had slept in that bed before him, he would likely have forced himself to sleep in the truck. It wasn't that he was a germaphobe or anything, he just hated motels.

He stared at the stained ceiling and listened to his stomach growl. Plower had taken off minutes before in search of dinner, leaving Tate alone to gather his thoughts. The kidnappings had occupied so much of his time over the previous weeks, he couldn't believe that this little town could hold the key that might bring this nightmare to an end.

Tate couldn't believe the sheriff was being so difficult to work with, but in a way he understood. This case was Mader's chance to get his name out there and prove to everyone that he was a force to be reckoned with. Tate respected that, and that was the only reason he was lying on a dingy comforter in a small-town motel.

The sheriff's thoughts were interrupted by the door opening and Plower entering the room with a bag in his left hand, drinks in his right, and another bag dangling from his mouth. He walked into the room, and dropped the bags on the vacant bed next to Tate's and sighed.

"I don't know what people do in this town for fun, but obviously going out to eat isn't much of an option," Plower commented as he kicked of his boots.

Tate sat up in bed and threw his legs over the edge. "Well, it smells good. What is it?"

"I got cheeseburgers and fries from the diner down the street. Smells good, but I can feel my arteries already starting to harden."

"Food's food," Tate chuckled as he grabbed one of the bags off the bed and released the burger from its aluminum-foil prison.

The men ate in silence and were both started by the phone ringing. Plower was sitting closest to the phone, and answered it. After a short conversation filled with "uh-huh" and "ok," he placed the receiver back on the antique base and turned his attention to Tate.

"Stephen's ready to talk."

<u>42</u>

"Why are you in Alabama at a time like this," Rob asked, more confused than angry. "All hell's breaking loose up here."

Carrie knew what she did was a bad idea, wrong even, but she offered no excuses for her behavior. "I just had some business I had to take care of here, Rob. I know you don't understand, but you are just going to have to believe me when I tell you it was unavoidable."

Silence. Even though he was hundreds of miles away, Carrie could see the frown lines digging deep in his forehead. "Look, Rob," she said softly, "I'm not quitting on this case. I'm in it for the long haul, but I needed to step away, if even for a few hours. I'm leaving here in about an hour. We'll meet at my place and head over to Millersville."

Silence again. "Say something," Carrie nearly whispered. Please, she begged silently.

"Please hurry," he finally said, sounding defeated. He knew arguing was pointless, because he wasn't going to get his way. Rob wanted to grab her through the phone and shake her. He wanted to scream at her and make her understand that she wasn't the only one who was suffering through this case; but, he didn't. He simply said his goodbyes and cried into his hands, the way he had done nights before when reality became too much.

Carrie gently closed her cell phone and gathered her composure. The conversation had forced her to leave the mobile home so she could talk private. She knew she wasn't being fair to Rob by leaving, but she really needed to get her heart back into the hunt, and her mama was the one who could get her on track.

She walked back into the trailer and sat down on the couch. Her mother walked in seconds later wearing a pair of shorts and a t-shirt and carrying a drink in each hand. She handed one to Carrie, and took a long drink before sitting down next to her daughter. Carrie took a sip and felt the alcohol burn its way down her throat.

"So, who was that on the phone? Boyfriend?"

Carrie's mother was raised in the South, and believed that women were put on Earth to get married and make babies. Carrie had heard that her whole life. So, when she came home with her acceptance letter from Vanderbilt in her hand, her mother was not happy. "Boys don't like girls who are too smart," she had reminded Carrie. With degree in hand, mama was still hell-bent on making sure her daughter found a boyfriend, because she was ready for grandbabies. "I don't want to be too old to enjoy them," she often joked. Carrie knew she was serious.

"No, mama. It's a guy I work with. His name is Rob, and we are investigating the Nashville kidnappings." She set her drink on the end table and folded her arms. "You know, mama, I'm working on my first major story. My boss thinks this is the one that could pay off for me. It's a tough story – real emotional."

Debra also set her drink down and grabbed both Carrie's hands in her own. "Baby, I'm so proud of you. So, what's he like? Is he cute?"

Carrie snatched her hands away and stood up. "Is he cute? Is that all you can think about? Is that all you heard? I just told you I'm doing well at my job … that I'm working on a major story, and you want to know what Rob looks like?" She spun around, grabbed her purse off the floor next to the recliner, and marched toward the front door. "I knew I never should have come back here," Carrie screamed before slamming the door behind her.

Once she reached the car, she threw her purse in the back seat, got behind the wheel and started the engine. Her anger burned her cheeks, and she turned the air conditioner on high and placed her forehead on the steering wheel, letting the cold are blow directly on her cheeks. The brisk air helped sooth her, inside and out. In that moment, she felt like a teenager after one of her daily fights with her mother. She was angry and hurt, and just wanted to run away like she had done years ago.

A knock on the car window drew her attention, and her rage. "I don't want to talk about it, Mom," she yelled without raising her head.

"Good, 'cause I don't want to talk about it either," a voice that was not her mother's answered. Carrie raised her head and turned to face her brother standing shoeless on the gravel next to the vehicle. "It's time we had a talk."

Carrie stepped out of the car and fell into the outreached arms of her brother. She could not remember the last time they had shown affection towards each other, but she knew it had been much too long. They didn't say anything for a while, just held each other tight.

"I have to go, Jake," Carrie finally said, pushing herself off his shoulder and wiping the tears from her eyes.

"You got big things to attend to, huh?"

"Sort of. Working on a pretty big story."

Jake leaned against the car and stared off into the distance with dreaming eyes Carrie hadn't seen since she was a little girl. "They got any jobs up in Nashville?" he asked without turning to look at his sister.

"Maybe," Carrie replied, unable to contain her smile. She knew what her brother was thinking.

"You think an Alabama hick like me could get one of those jobs?"

Carrie looked at her big brother, and noticed that he had showered and shaved. He was wearing a crisp, clean button-up shirt and blue jeans. "I got one. If I can, you can."

"I don't know about that," he said with a crooked smile. "You have a college degree and a lot of brains. I barely graduated from high school."

Carrie turned and faced her brother. "Go get your bag, Jake. Let's go … get the hell out of this town and face the world together."

Jake looked at the house and then toward his sister. "I can't. I can't leave Mom. You know how it is."

The screen door shut and the siblings turned to see their mother holding a duffle bag, her other hand covering the lower part of her face, tears streaming. She walked out to the car, placed the bag down, and looked up to her son. "You call me, Jacob Ryan Stevens, and let me know you're ok every once and a while." She grabbed her son in a bear hug, squeezed him tight, and turned toward her daughter.

"And you need to keep in touch more, too, young lady. Grown up or not, you are still my baby girl." She hugged Carrie and quickly walked to the trailer.

Without knowing what to say, brother and sister got into the car and began the silent drive to Eastern Tennessee.

Stephen had hoped he would be taken to a small room with two-way mirrors with a small table sitting in the middle of the room. Instead, he was sitting by himself in an empty office. There was a desk in the room and several chairs, but that was it. No mirrors.

He was sitting there, slowly sipping a soda when the sheriff and another man walked into the room. Introductions were made, and the stranger was identified as Sheriff Tate from Nashville. He reached out his hand for Stephen to shake, and sat down across the table from the youngster.

"Stephen, it is a pleasure to meet you," Tate started, smiling yet serious. "Sounds like you have been through quite an ordeal."

"Yes sir."

"Would you mind telling me about it?"

Stephen stared intently at his soda can. "What do you want to know?"

Tate leaned back in the old, wooden chair and crossed his legs. "How about just starting from the beginning?"

Stephen's voice shook as he told the story, but the more he got involved in it, the easier the words came. "I was in the park playing. We were playing Ninja, and I was looking for a great place to hide. I found this tree on the edge of the park and started climbing it."

"Who were you playing Ninja with?"

"Ryan. He's my best friend. He's real good at finding me when I'm hiding, plus, I'm afraid of heights, so I knew he would never look up in a tree for me. So, that's why I climbed the tree."

"But, weren't you afraid to climb it?"

"Well, when you're trying to win a game, sometimes you gotta do things you don't want to. I was afraid, but I knew if I climbed it, I would win. So I climbed it. I got about halfway up and sat on a branch waiting for Ryan to come. I could hear him calling my name but he was far away."

"How long were you in the tree, Stephen?"

"A few minutes before it started cracking. I felt it start to give way, so I grabbed onto the trunk of the tree. Just in time, too, cause just after I did that, the tree branch fell."

"Wow. That was some quick thinking by you," Tate said in an exaggerated voice. When the boy's chest puffed out and a grin came over his face, Tate knew it was working. "So, how did you get out of the tree?"

Stephen leaned back in the chair and started swinging his thin legs, the heel of his tennis shoe made a hollow thump as it hit the leg of the chair. "I stayed there for a few minutes. I thought about yelling for help, but I knew Ryan would hear me, and I sure didn't want him to see me like that. Then I heard talking behind me."

"Who was talking behind you?"

"There was a man and woman arguing in their front yard, and I think that is what I heard, but then there was a voice below me. Some guy was standing there. He asked if I needed help and held up his hands like he would catch me. I was too afraid to think about dropping, but then I started losing my grip."

Tate noticed that Stephen's face was starting to show fear, which meant he was right there, on that exact day, reliving the events. Aluminum crackled as the boy's young hands gripped the soda can tightly. "Keep going Stephen. What happened next?"

"I fell. I felt the man catch me before I hit the ground, and then I started crying."

"What did the man do?"

"He was nice. He asked me if I was ok, and then we walked over to his car. I had a scrape on my leg, and he said he had a Band-Aid in his car."

Stupid kid, thought Tate. How many times had he been warned in school, and probably from his parents, to stay away from strangers? Why did he not heed the advice?

"So, when I got there, he gave me a Band-Aid. I felt something go over my face, and the next thing I knew, I was in a dark room with Thomas."

"Do you remember what he looked like?"

"I never saw his face."

"Do you remember what he was wearing the day he helped you in the   park?"

Stephen shook his head no, and that was the end of the conversation. He didn't want to talk anymore about the situation, and there wasn't a damn thing Tate could do about it. The sheriff stood up, thanked Stephen, and told him he would be back the following day to talk to him some more.

When he stepped into the hallway and closed the door to the office so Stephen couldn't hear him, he turned to Sheriff Mader. "I want to transfer this boy to Nashville. There is no need for him to remain here."

Mader ran his fingers along his handlebar moustache and smiled. "We'll see," he said smugly before turning his back to Tate and walking to his office.

<u>43</u>

L andon didn't know what to say to E.J. He wanted to go home, too, but the thought of leaving the cabin and trying to find someone to help them was overwhelmingly scary. The tiny house was surrounded by thick, haunting woods as far as the eye could see. Even if he was confident in his ability to survive in the brush, he certainly wasn't able to take care of another kid. That would be suicide.

His thoughts were interrupted by the distant sound of a vehicle coming up the mountain. Landon ran to the front door and saw a pickup truck making its way up the dirt path towards the cabin. Landon could feel panic starting to take control. He turned and ran toward the back of the cabin, grabbing E.J.'s arm. They ran out the back door and hid in the underbrush behind the cabin as they had done before.

The dark green pickup truck came to a sliding halt in front of the cabin. Landon and E.J. slowly made their way toward the front so they could see, making sure to be quiet and hidden. Each crunch of leaves or breaking stick stopped the two boys in their tracks, and they continued only after making sure they had not drawn any attention.

The driver's door of the truck opened, and a set of worn, muddy boots emerged from inside. There were muffled voices coming from the cab of the vehicle, followed by a loud, "SHUT UP!" The owner of the boots emerged from the truck and slammed the door shut. It was a tall man wearing a dirty, gray t-shirt, and dirty jeans. His face was hidden by the bill of a Tennessee Titans cap and a full beard. He was big, and tall, and scary, Landon thought.

The man lumbered to the porch of the house and eventually went inside.

"Stay here," Landon whispered to E.J. before half crawling and half walking to the truck. Kneeling in the mud next to the truck, he opened the driver's door and motioned for E.J. to join him.

E.J. ran to the truck, and jumped in the cab. Two small children were sitting on the front seat, scrunched up against the passenger door, crying.

"Get down," Landon ordered the other children. He placed his hand on the key chain dangling from the ignition and turned the key. The truck roared to life as the front door of the cabin flew open and the man stood in the doorway sneering at the boy behind the wheel. Landon threw the vehicle in reverse and slid down in the seat so he could press the gas pedal to the floor. The truck spun its tires and stopped after hitting a tree with its rear bumper.

Landon turned to E.J. who had his eyes closed in terror. "Help me," Landon screamed.

Following Landon's instructions, E.J. got on the floor and placed both hands on the gas pedal.

The truck fish-tailed in the wet clay before finally gaining traction and speeding toward the house. Landon turned the steering wheel in an attempt to avoid another collision, and steered toward the road that wound its way down the mountain. He could hear the man screaming obscenities at him as the vehicle sped away.

Once Landon could see a paved road in the distance, he ordered E.J. to take his hands off the gas pedal, and the truck began to slow down, stopping in the middle of the paved road. All of the children exited the vehicle and went to the side of the road, each one crying tears of joy or fear. E.J. wrapped his arms around Landon in a silent "thank you."

Carrie and Jake pulled into Millersville and found a parking spot behind Rob's car in front of the town's motel. After making a quick call to her partner, brother and sister walked into the motel. The lobby was old and musty and hadn't been used in years. A dust film seemed to cover everything in the room. They slipped past the elderly woman asleep behind the front desk, and climbed the stairs to room 216. Rob was standing in front of the open door frame in a pair of jeans with no shirt or shoes. Wet hair told Carrie that he had just taken a shower.

She introduced Rob to Jake and plopped herself down on the queen-size bed in the middle of the room. The room was small, barely big enough to hold the bed and a dresser. A small t.v. took up the entire top of the dresser and was turned to a news channel. The walls were covered in faded paisley wallpaper that clashed with the orange, stained comforter on the bed. The carpet had been teal in its heyday, but time had turned it brown in spots and it was worn down to the concrete below.

Jake sat down next to his sister and leaned toward her. "He's cute," he whispered, nudging her arm. Carrie elbowed him in the ribs.

"So, what do we know," Carrie asked Rob.

"Well, the boy is at the sheriff's office and was interviewed by Tate about an hour ago. I learned that from the owner of the drug store, a Mr. Killen, who spends most of his time staring out the window and making notes on what is happening."

"Sounds like a nosey neighbor," Jake added.

Rob smiled. "More than nosey; he literally writes down what is happening in town in a little notebook he keeps in his pocket. A very … uh … interesting guy."

"Hello, Rain Man," Jake muttered, drawing a chuckle from everyone.

"We should see if we can get in to talk to the boy," Carrie offered.

Rob leaned against the wall and ran a comb through his long hair. "I think we would probably do better talking to Tate and seeing what he has to say. If we want to talk to the boy, he is the one that will be able to get us in."

Jake stood up and stretched. "I don't know about you all, but I am starving. We passed by a little diner down the street and I think I'm going to head there and get a burger. Anyone want to join me?"

As much as Carrie wanted to get started on the investigation, her rumbling stomach told her food was a great idea. Rob agreed, and the trio headed down the street to Marge's Diner.

Despite its rugged outside, the diner was clean and quaint. The trio found a table in the back of the dining room, ordered their drinks and browsed the menu. Besides the typical diner fare of hamburgers, deli sandwiches, and various salads, there were also dinner choices that promised to taste "just like mom made." While the selections of country fried steak and fried chicken seemed appealing, Carrie decided to skip the grease and ordered a chef's salad and a cup of chicken noodle soup. Rob ordered a cheeseburger with fries, and Jake wanted a club sandwich.

Carrie and Rob caught up on what was happening with the case, as Jake listened in. Once their stomachs were full, they headed out the door. The sun was setting, and the air was getting cooler, which suddenly made Carrie tired. Rob apparently noticed her drooping eyes. "Why don't you two go back to the motel and call it a day. I'll go talk to Tate and see if I can get something set up for tomorrow."

Carrie nodded in agreement and started her slow walk toward the motel. Jake asked to go with Rob, and was given an "ok" from Carrie who was struggling to keep from passing out. He wanted to meet the sheriff he had heard so much about.

The semi screeched to a stop, its tires leaving streaks of rubber as the driver tried to miss the pick-up truck sitting in the middle of the road. He was nearly successful, the bumper of his big rig barely tapping the rusty metal on the front of the truck.

Mumbling obscenities, the driver hopped out of the semi and walked to the pickup ready to pummel whoever was inside, only to find an empty cab. A quick glance around and he noticed the small face in the thick brush next to the road. He placed his hands on his hips and exhaled. "Well, come on out," he said harshly in his thick Southern accent.

Landon didn't know what to do. The man was what his sister would call gruff-looking. His jeans were held up under his protruding belly by suspenders. He wore old work boots and a white t-shirt. His pudgy, rough face was covered in a beard. Though he had what appeared to be kind eyes, he was chomping on a cigar and talked in hoarse voice that made Landon leery.

"Don't go out there," E.J. pleaded, holding on tightly to Landon's arm.

"It'll be ok, E.J.. I promise. If the man wanted to hurt us, he would have done it by now. I think he wants to talk, and maybe he can help us."

"What if he doesn't want to talk? What if he wants to hurt you?"

"Then you take these kids and you run into the woods as fast as you can. Don't you stop or look back until your legs won't let you run anymore. You understand me?"

E.J. nodded his head and swiped the beginnings of a tear from his eye.

Landon pried the boy's fingers from his flesh, stood and walked apprehensively toward the road. He tried not to look like the scared little puppy he felt like. When he reached the edge of the pavement he stopped.

"This your truck?" the man asked jerking his head in the direction of the pickup.

Landon shook his head from side to side. He was being honest. It wasn't his truck, though he was obviously the one who left it there.

"Where's your mom or dad? They need to come get this outta the way. I got a delivery to make."

"They aren't here."

The man threw the cigar butt on the pavement and ground it with his boot. He reached into his pocket and pulled out a packet of chewing tobacco. He showed a handful of the brown, leafy concoction in his mouth without taking his eyes off Landon. "So, it looks like we have a mess on our hands, doesn't it?"

Landon could feel a terror tremble begin to form in his chest and slowly work its way to his arms and legs. "Sir … I … I … don't know what you want me to say." As much as he wanted to sound like a confident man, he knew at that moment, in the eyes of the truck driver, he was just a scared little boy. He shoved his hands deep in his pockets and began to finger little pieces of lint gathering at the seam.

The truck driver spit a stream of brown liquid, and wiped his mouth with the back of his arm. "Why don't we start with your name and why this truck is in the middle of the road."

Landon found himself back in 2nd grade, listening to his teacher Mrs. Horace and that really cool deputy from the Sheriff's Office reminding him of "stranger danger." Over and over the phrase played in his head. "We … I accidentally stalled the truck in the road and couldn't get it to start again."

The man shook his head. "Why were you driving? What are you … 12 … 13?"

Landon looked at the ground and nodded. What could he say?

Silence encompassed the scene like a blanket. Neither person spoke, neither knowing what to say. Finally, in the softest voice Landon had ever heard, the man spoke. "Are you in some kind of trouble, son?"

Landon nodded his head. All of the fear, anxiousness, desperation, and pain that had encompassed him for so long finally released him, and he spilled everything on the shocked man. After talking for what seemed like hours, Landon's voice silenced and the enormous weight he had been carrying lifted. He turned towards the woods and motioned for E.J. and the others to join him.

Apprehensively, the children walked to the road and stood around Landon. The driver smiled and put his arm around the young man, and without a word being spoken, Landon felt safe.

44

Carrie wasn't sure what Rob and Jake had said or done during their visit with the Sheriff, but whatever they did worked, and within 24 hours of arriving in Millersville, all three were sitting in the small Sheriff's Office waiting to talk to Stephen.

The office was small, but took up the entire bottom floor of an old, wooden building in the heart of downtown. A large counter ran the length of the room and blocked people from entering the main part of the office except through a small gate at the end. A large woman sat behind the counter and seemed to type endlessly on an old, manual typewriter. She looked to be in her late 60s and answered to the name "Lucille."

The room was actually a small office, and it looked nothing like Carrie pictured; of course, her images were from police shows on t.v. and the big screen. There was not a two-way mirror with a group of sarcastic police officers behind it watching them. There was not a big wooden table with two chairs where the boy would be handcuffed to the table during the conversation.

It was just an office, with pictures of past law enforcement officers decorating the dull, cinder-block walls. A window with blinds drawn sat across from the door, and a small, wooden desk with a calendar and telephone on it sat in a corner.

The trio sat in silence until the door opened and a boy walked in timidly. He looked exactly like the picture that Carrie had burned into her memory. She was so happy to see him, yet she didn't even know him.

Stephen walked to the desk and sat down, his small frame seemingly swallowed by a faux-leather chair.

Carrie walked over, sat across from him, and introduced everyone in the room. "We met your parents," she added with a smile. "They have been very worried about you and will be glad to see you."

If the statement had any effect on the boy, it did not show in his face, which was tense and frowning. "When can I see them?"

"The Sheriff's office is working on getting them out here to pick you up," Rob responded.

"Stephen," Carrie asked in a gentle voice, "can you tell us about what happened to you?"

The child looked around as if he just became aware of his surroundings and of the strangers in the room. "I think I need a lawyer," he said in a voice cracking with fear.

Carrie could see that Jake was stifling a chuckle, and she gave him a look that prompted him to get up and excuse himself from the room. She then turned her attention back to Stephen. "Honey, the only people who need attorneys are those who are in trouble or being accused of being in trouble. You are neither."

The boy looked down at his hands and began interlocking his fingers. He said nothing, but his body was screaming fear.

Carrie touched his arm. "We are not here to accuse you of anything," she said. "We are just trying to find out what happened, who did it, and why."

Still no response from the boy, and after waiting for what seemed like hours, Carrie rose to her feet and tussled Stephen's hair. "We are going to give you some time to think, and we will be back tomorrow. I would really like to talk to you, and I hope you will consider doing the same." Though she tried to keep her tone friendly, Carrie knew the words were coming out with a bit of a bite, and she prayed that Stephen wasn't frightened away.

Rob opened the door and stepped into the hallway, and Carrie was about to do the same when she heard a faint noise coming from the youngster. She turned. "What?"

"Just you," he repeated without looking up from his hands. "Come tomorrow, just you, and we'll talk."

Rob seemed offended when Carrie revealed what Stephen had said. "Why can't he talk to all of us," he asked to no one in particular? He kicked an imaginary rock on the sidewalk and threw his hands in the air. "This is bullshit."

"Rob, I don't think it has anything to do with you."

Rob continued walking, ignoring what she was saying. Maybe she was just tired, but the sound of his shoes hitting the dirty sidewalk paired with his mumbling crawled under Carrie's skin and made her irritable. She stopped mid track, hands on hips and waited for him to notice. It took a few minutes before he turned around and yelled "what!" in a voice so loud that the building walls seemed to tremble.

"I don't think Stephen's decision has anything to do with you."

"Oh really? Then why? Why does he want to meet with just you?"

"Why are you acting like this?" Carrie walked to his side and lowered her voice. "This is the decision of a child, and you know I'm going to share what he says. Why does it matter whether it's me or you he talks to?"

Rob's shoulders sank with the weight of the world. "I've been here, Carrie, just like you. I've waded through the mounds of emotional shit we've faced, just like you. But, I didn't run away like you."

The statement hit her like a ton of bricks. She never realized that she had made him feel that way. In fact, she had never even thought about his feelings, only hers. But what right did he have to say that? She didn't run away, she left. There was a difference, and damn him for not seeing that. Sadness and anger seemed to cover her like a stiff blanket on a warm evening. Her face felt hot, and her shock was suddenly replaced by the anger that comes with embarrassment.

"I did not run away, Rob. Damn you for saying that.'

"Really," Rob questioned mockingly, "then what was it? What do you call it when a person leaves in the middle of an investigation to go visit relative hundreds of miles away ... A vacation?"

Carrie turned on her heels and stomped away. His calls for her to return were responded to with an increase of speed. She was done ... over. Harlan could take his money and shove it up his ass for all she cared.

"Carrie, stop," Rob ordered grabbing her arm in an effort to get her to listen. She pulled away from him and broke into a half walk/half jog.

"I'm sorry," he yelled from the sidewalk just before she turned into the motel and disappeared.

45

All of the children piled into the cab of the semi-truck and sat perfectly still, partially in fear and partially in relief. E.J. had chosen to sit on the floor and was holding onto Landon's leg with one arm, and sucking on his thumb. Landon still didn't trust the driver, but at this point, it didn't matter.

The ride was bumpy, long and boring. There were houses sprinkled on the mountain sides along the small, two-lane road, but for the most part, the view out the window was nothing but trees and mountain valleys. The crackles of the CB radio, the shifting of gears and the whistling of the wind through the partially-opened windows were almost melodic.

The driver waited nearly an hour before trying to make conversation. "So, where are you from, kid?"

Landon, not sure if he was the one being addressed, noticed that the other children were sleeping, and answered, "Nashville"

"You're a long way from home."

"Where are we?" Landon asked.

The driver downshifted as the truck struggled up a steep incline and finally answered once the vehicle crested the hill. "Well, we're about an hour northwest of Gatlinburg, heading west. We'll be in the town of Millersville in about 15 minutes."

"Where's Gatlinburg?"

"Son, we're about four hours away from Nashville. I don't know how you got all the way out here alone, but I reckon you'll be back home in a matter of hours."

A sudden wave of emotion overtook Landon and he began to cry silently. He wasn't sad or relieved. It seemed as if everything that had happened to him over the past few weeks had turned into a flood of tears that were pouring out of his eyes. Normally, he would have been embarrassed, but this was not a normal day.

Stephen was lying on the small cot in the jail cell lost in thought when the slamming door of another cell down the hall snapped him back into reality. He wasn't sad or afraid anymore. He just wanted to go home.

He couldn't explain why he trusted the reporter lady he met earlier, but he did. She seemed really nice and spoke in a soft voice that reminded him of his mother's before the demons took her over and made her mean. He wanted to spill his guts to the lady, but he wasn't quite sure if he could trust her. The last grown-up he trusted shoved him into a car and put a smelly rag over his face. When he woke, he was in a dark, stinky room with a crying boy. But, there was something about her.

A guard tapped on the cell and slid a tray under the barred door. His name was Freddie, and he was quiet but kind. Stephen picked at the food, but couldn't bring himself to eat more than a nibble at a time. His stomach was in knots. He finally gave up and lay back down on the cot fighting to keep the little bit of food he ate down. He was ready to go home.

Rob found Carrie in the motel room packing her bags. He walked in and sat down on the bed adjacent to hers watching her. He couldn't help but notice how attractive she was when she was angry. He also couldn't help but notice how dangerous she was, either. He waited on her to say something, but she didn't.

"I said I was sorry," he offered kindly.

"I heard you." Her tone was sharp.

Silence.

"Where are you going?"

"What do you care?"

"Umm … we're a team?"

That did it. Carrie threw a pair of jeans in the bag as hard as she could and glared at Rob, her face growing as red as a beet. "I saw that teamwork, Rob, when Stephen dared to want to talk me instead of you. Suddenly, it wasn't about this case anymore, it was about poor Rob and how mean Carrie has been." Stripes of anger began flowing down her cheeks. She was so tired of crying, yet didn't know how to stop. She plopped down on the bed, hard, sending her suitcase to the floor. Though her back was to him, Rob could tell she was still upset.

He got up and walked around her bed and kneeled on the floor in front of her. He wiped the tears from her warm cheeks and then held her hands. "I'm sorry. I didn't mean that and I don't think you're mean. I think you are one of the most amazing women I've ever met."

Carrie looked up with red eyes and smiled. "No you don't."

"You're right. You're really a big bitch," he said sarcastically as he leaned forward and gently kissed her running his hands through her hair, and before either of them knew it, they were making love.

Carrie was awakened by the sound of someone running down the hall and knocking on her door. "Carrie, it's Jake. Let's go. Something's going on at the Sheriff's Office."

She sat up in bed and woke up Rob. Within fifteen minutes all three of them joined Sheriff Tate in the lobby of the Sheriff's Office watching as Landon, E.J., Billy's children, Miranda and Willie, and a man Carrie had never seen before were led into the building by smiling Sheriff Mader and two deputies. The adults were summoned to a large conference room at the back of the police station and were joined there by Mader.

"Ok, folks," Mader started, "here's what we are going to do. The parents of the children have been notified and will be picking up their children here at the station Friday. That's day after tomorrow. An official press release will be sent to media locally and in Nashville tomorrow, Wednesday." He then turned his sights on Carrie, Rob and Jake. "No interviews will be given unless they are Ok'd by the parents. We have this matter under control. Any questions will be referred to our information officer, Deputy Kyle Roland." Mader placed his hand on a young uniformed man standing next to him. "Thank you," he finished before walking out of the room, deputies in tow.

Within minutes, Carrie, Rob, and Jake were the only ones left sitting at the oversized table. Rob ran his hands over his face in aggravation, his beard stubble making a sandpaper sound. "This is ridiculous," he finally said in an exhausted voice.

Carrie nodded in agreement.

"How much you wanna bet there wasn't an information officer in this Podunk town before this morning?" Jake added with a chuckle.

"Well, I guess we can get out of here for now," Rob said, pushing his chair back and rising. "It's a sure bet Mader isn't going to let us near those boys."

The trio walked out of the room and back to the motel. Jake said he was tired and was going back to bed. Carrie and Rob decided to take a ride through the area and take in the scenery. Chances were not much was going to happen until Friday, or so they thought.

Landon knew it was all going to be ok. The minute they pulled into the small town he couldn't keep the smile off his face. The only thing that would have made it better would have been seeing his family waiting for him, but he knew that was no longer a dream.

The tru   ck stopped in front of a large brick building Next to the door were two large pane windows with "Sheriff's Office" stenciled on the front in gold letters. The driver got out and spoke with a man in uniform who promptly went inside and returned with two more uniformed men, one who opened the passenger door.

"Hi everyone," he began in a voice that seemed much too high for a man's voice. "My name is Deputy Holland. We are going to go inside the Sheriff's office where we will talk a little bit, and then we will be calling your family so you can go home. How does that sound?"

The children seemed to light up with the news, while Landon felt his back straighten and his shoulders drop back as he listened to the sing-song tone of the deputy's voice which sounded like he was talking to a group of 1st graders. They were then herded into the Sheriff's office and placed in separate rooms from each other.

Landon sat in a large, noisy chair that was probably a hand-me-down or discarded to make room for a new chair in someone's office. The room smelled musty, like it hadn't been used in a long time, and the layer of dust on the window sill and table confirmed his suspicions.

It was at this moment that Landon noticed his reflection in the hazy window. His hair was matted to his head and filthy. He had put the brand-new t-shirt on the morning he was taken, and his cutoffs were brown with dirt. His mother would be upset to see him in that state and he wondered if he would be able to take a shower and wash his clothes before he saw her. He had upset her enough and didn't want to cause her more tears.

He had been sitting in the room for nearly an hour and was scraping clay off the sides of his tennis shoes with his dirty fingernails when the deputy who was talking to the driver came in the room.

"Hello. My name is Sheriff Mader, and you are?" the man said with breath that smelled like wintergreen life savers.

"Landon."

"Hi, Landon. It seems like you have quite a story to tell."

The boy squirmed in his chair uncomfortably and took great interest in a spot of dirt on his shirt.

Silence engulfed the room for nearly 20 minutes before Mader rose to his feet. He explained to Landon that he would give him the night to think things over, and when they reconvened in the morning, he made it clear that he expected some answers. Landon simply nodded in a child-like manner, never once making eye contact.

Deputy Holland found talking to E.J. easy. The youngster was quick to explain what had happened to him and could describe in detail usually not provided from such young witnesses. Holland struggled to keep up with his writing, wishing he had remembered a recorder. He was not about to stop the boy's story to have someone fetch one for him. He could feel his hand start to cramp when the boy ended a sentence and sat quietly for a moment. "I guess that's all," E.J. smiled.

Holland finished writing, ordered the boy to remain seated, and quickly made his way to the sheriff's office.   His hands were trembling with the excitement of dealing with his first big case.

Mader had just sat down in his chair and was rubbing his temples in frustration when Holland burst through the office door. He was about to admonish the young deputy and speak to him about knocking, but one look at the deputy's face let the sheriff know something big was happening.

"I know where this place is," the deputy nearly screamed at the sheriff, his face red from the excitement.

"Sit down Holland, and calm down."

The deputy's face fell in disappointment as he sat gingerly on the chair in front of the sheriff's cluttered desk.

"Ok," Mader said in a calm voice, "what is going on?"

"I want to go back to the Sheriff's Office," Carrie said while looking out the window. She was oblivious to the scenery; the case had literally taken over her life.

"He's not going to tell us anything," Rob said as he pulled on the shoulder of the small mountain road.

"If we sit there long enough, someone is going to have to say something just to get us out of the way." She pleaded with Rob with eyes glazed over by determination. "Let's be the squeaky wheel, dammit."

Without saying a word, Rob agreed as he turned the car around and headed back to town. He was ready to move on with his life.

Stephen stared at the ceiling from his cot. A small drip from the sink in the back of the cell was more soothing than it was annoying. The aroma of his dinner still lingered in the air, making him feel more like he was at home than in a jail.

He did not want to talk to the police men anymore, and he wasn't going to. What was it called, he tried to remember, when people couldn't make you say something you didn't want to? Pleading the … something. He was going to do that. They couldn't make him talk anymore … could they?

<u>46</u>

Carrie and Rob had been sitting in the small foyer of the Sheriff's Office for hours when they were finally called back by the sheriff.

"I don't know what you all think you are going to get out of me, but I'm not going to talk to you anymore about this case until I talk to the parents." Mader smiled a satisfied smile, leaned back in his chair and put a wad of chewing tobacco in his mouth.

"You talked to us before, why do things have to change," Carrie asked.

"Because things have changed. We weren't caught up in this media circus like we are now."

"Which should be more of a reason to talk to us," Rob interjected. "We can help you. We're not here to steal your thunder, Sheriff, we are just trying to do our jobs, just like you are."

The conversation was interrupted by a ringing phone. Mader answered, and hung up. He stood, grabbed his hat and excused himself. "I'll be right back."

Another positioned himself outside the office door, and they both knew it was to keep an eye on them. That is when Carrie noticed the legal pad on the desk. As inconspicuously as possible, she strained her neck to read the writing. His interest peaked when she said E.J.'s name.

"Distract the deputy," she leaned back and whispered to her partner while nodding her head toward the desk. Rob nodded in agreement and stood.

"Hey, where's the bathroom," he said as he headed to the office door. He positioned himself between the officer and the office window giving Carrie just enough time to tear several sheets of paper off the pad and shove them in her pocket.

"Forget it, Rob," she said as she headed to the hallway. "They aren't going to talk to us anymore. Let's just go."

Rob headed to the bathroom and Carrie made her way out of the building, passing the sheriff who was talking to a reporter. He tipped his hat at her as she put on a fake scowl and headed to the motel.

Rob arrived in the room within minutes of Carrie, and they bother scoured the paper looking for info. Their hearts skipped a beat when they saw what appeared to be directions and an address written on the back of the second page.

"Let's go," Rob said, grabbing Carrie's arm and nearly dragging her out of the room.

Jake awoke from his nap, and for a minute, he didn't know where he was. He sat up quickly, and focused, realizing he was in a motel room. He splashed some water on his face, buttoned his shirt and headed to the Sheriff's Office to find out what his sister was doing.

47

The sun was just beginning to set when Carrie and Rob reached the narrow, dirt driveway that lead to the cabin. Rob was concerned about trying to navigate the steep grade in the dark, but Carrie was persistent. They had come this far, and there was no turning back.

The Jeep's tires slid on the muddy terrain and when it seemed Rob was about to lose control, the four-wheel-drive kicked in and found traction. Carrie white-knuckled the roll bar and closed her eyes, praying as the Jeep slowly climbed the mountain. By the time they reached the top, the stars were shining brightly in the pitch-black sky, and the cabin was spotlighted by the moon.

Carrie opened the glove compartment and grabbed a flashlight. The windows in the cabin were dark, and the only life in the area was the crackling of the deer walking in the forest and the occasional call of the coyote and hoot of the owl. She stepped out of the Jeep quietly and began making her way to the front door with Rob following closely. The weather-worn porch boards creaking under their weight caused them to pause nervously, and they waited to see if anyone heard; but the deafening chorus of crickets made it clear that they were alone.

The front door was ajar, and the cabin was dark. Rob opened the door slowly and took soft, deliberate steps into the dwelling. The living room was bare and there was no heat indicating that a fire had been built recently in the fireplace. They checked every room in the cabin and found each eerily empty. It looked and felt as if no one had been there for years.

Carrie tried to imagine a group of children being holed up in this little cabin and the fear they must have felt not knowing what was going to happen to them. The musty smell of the wood probably suffocated them with fear. Was there even running water here?

They made their way back to the front of the cabin and stopped in the middle of the living room. "Well, this was a waste of …" Rob began, his words cut off by a horrifying cracking sound. Carrie threw her hands up to her mouth to stifle a scream while Rob looked pleadingly into her eyes.

"Rob?" Her question was stopped as he looked up to the ceiling, a single line of red trickling from his hairline into his right eye. Rob collapsed to his knees, and then fell forward onto Carrie's legs, knocking her down. By the time the two bodies hit the floor, Rob's body was lifeless.

Startled, Carrie quickly regained her composure and looked where Rob was standing; a dark shadow blocked the moonlight in the doorway. She tried to push Rob off, but he was too heavy to move. She was defenseless.

The figure entered the cabin and closed the door hard. Carrie could see a shadow moving around the room, and within minutes a fire blazed in the fireplace. Carrie gasped as the man turned and revealed a very familiar face.

"What do you mean you let them go? Where are they?" Jake screamed as he grabbed the collar of the young sheriff's deputy and pinned him against the wall.

"I … I didn't LET them go. They just left," the officer stammered. He looked like he was about to cry as Jake struggled to regain his composure and let go of the man's clothing. He sat down in front of the sheriff's desk and put his face in his hands.

"I'll call the Sheriff," the deputy said as he quickly ran from the room.

Jake looked up to the ceiling waiting for some sort of divine intervention, and when none arrived, he gazed at the desk in front of him. A lone file folder sat open on top of a desk calendar. Jake stood up and grabbed the folder. It was a piece of paper obviously written by a child describing what had happened to him. A yellow post-it note sat on top of the paper with an address. Jake grabbed the note and ran out of the building.

Carrie's scream was stifled by a large hand covering her mouth and the blade of a large knife inches from her face. He leaned in so close to her face that she could feel the heat from his breath on her cheeks.

"I'm going to take my hand away. We are alone out here, so if I hear another sound from you …" he twisted the knife closer to her eyes. "Do you understand?" A deep voice growled.

Carrie nodded yes and felt a tear work its way down her face.

The man grabbed Rob by the back collar of his shirt and roughly tossed him to the side like he was weightless. Carrie felt the coolness as the air hit a large spot of blood that formed on her pants where Rob's head had been. She couldn't look over at his body for fear he was dead.

The man walked back to tend to the fire and ordered Carrie to sit on the couch near the fireplace.

"I take it by your reaction that you know who I am." The man was kneeling in front of the fireplace breaking twigs and tossing them into the blaze. Each sound of bark breaking made Carrie jump.

She nodded. "You're Mark Proffit, Harlan's nephew."

The man turned toward her, his eyes burning through her. "And you're Carrie Stevens from the newspaper."

She could feel a shiver starting at her neck and clawing its way down her spine. The newspaper had not been kind to Proffit when he was running for councilman. An editorial had called him Harlan's pawn while endorsing Billy. When Election Day came, Proffit had received a mere 12 percent of the vote; he did not go down graciously. He voiced his disdain to everyone who would listen, boycotted the *News*, and, it was rumored, spent every dime he had putting up billboards around Nashville before finally disappearing.

Carrie couldn't help but wonder if this was all a setup from the beginning. Did Harlan arrange to have these children kidnapped in some sort of publicity stunt? No, she thought. Even Harlan's not that evil. Besides, it was well known by most Nashvillians that Harlan was embarrassed by his nephew's actions during and after the election.

"So, Carrie, what brings you out to this neck of the woods?" Proffit asked with a chuckle.

"Why did you do it, Mr. Proffit. Why did you take these kids? Was it because of Harlan?"

Yet again, the mention of Harlan's name seemed to draw out the demons. Proffit stood swiftly and threw off his coat. He was a tall, slender man who had obviously been living in the cabin for a while. His dark, flannel shirt had not seen a washing machine in some time, and neither had his dirty jeans. His face bore a weeks-old beard and his eyes were sunken in and tired.

He grabbed a hunting knife from a sheath attached to his belt and rush over to Carrie, pinning her on the couch with his left forearm across her neck, and the hunting knife aimed at her face. "Don't you ever mention that man's name in here again."

Jake found Carrie's car keys in her purse on the desk in the motel room. She rarely carried her purse when she was working, and he was glad that was one of those times. Once he got into the small car, he found a map of the state under the passenger's seat and tried to locate where this address was. It made no sense to him, and he was about to get out and find someone when a small face appeared in the window. "I know where it is," the young man opened the passenger's door. "Let's go."

Carrie closed her eyes and waited for the blade to strike her, but it did not come. When she looked again, Proffit was falling backwards, being pulled by a bloodied Rob. They both hit the floor with a hard crash causing Rob to get the wind knocked out of him. The knife flew across the room.

Proffit was the first to get to his feet, which terrified Carrie. She jumped from the couch and ran to the spot she thought the weapon had landed, only to be knocked away by Proffit's fist striking her back. Her breath oozed from her lungs in a loud wheeze, as she tried desperately to catch her breath. He fumbled around for the knife and finally located it, turning his attention to Carrie once again. She lost count at how many times the blade rose and fell toward her, but each swipe missed its intended target and left trenches of pain on her arms.

The melee was halted once again by Rob, who had regained his whereabouts and tackled Proffit. Carrie struggled to keep conscious, but each minute made her eyelids draw heavier, and then the world turned black.

<u>48</u>

The young detective called Sheriff Mader's phone about 20 times before he gave up. He was standing on the sidewalk without a clue what to do when he saw Sheriff Tate walking toward the office.

He screamed for the sheriff's attention and ran to catch up. "Sir, I'm Deputy Kilroy, and we have a situation."

The boy was Landon, and he had been observant during his ride with the truck driver. Within an hour Jake came around a bend in the highway and saw the old pickup that Landon had wrecked.

"There's got to be a driveway somewhere past here to get up to the house," the boy said to Jake, and he was right. About a half mile down the road was the small, dirt driveway making its way up the mountain to the cabin. Jake knew the car wouldn't be able to take the climb, so he pulled the car on the side of the road and the two began climbing.

Pain drew Carrie back to life, and when she opened her eyes, she was sitting upright on the couch. Her arms were stiff with blood and wrapped in towels. A noise behind her drew her attention, and within minutes, Proffit was in front of her dragging Rob's lifeless body by his ankles.

"So glad you are awake,' he said. His mouth was bloodied and his upper lip was split. The knife was back in its sheath. "I wouldn't want you to miss this."

Proffit sat Rob up and leaned him against the wall. A small groan from her friend sent a feeling of relief through her body. Once he positioned Rob where he wanted him, Proffit sat cross-legged on the floor and faced Carrie. He pulled the knife out and began witling a piece of twig.

"You ruined my life," he finally said in a voice barely above a whisper.

"No …"

"You … you people, can't just leave well enough alone, can you? You couldn't just leave it alone that I was related to that bastard. You had to keep bringing it up, acting like I even spoke to him. He is nothing to me, but no one knew that. There was no way I was going to win that election." He jumped up in a rush, grabbed Carrie by the hair on both sides of the face and pushed her into the back of the couch. "Because of you," he snarled with his face no more than an inch away from hers.

Fear and pain kept Carrie from speaking or crying. She felt as if she were frozen in time. Proffit finally let her go, and turned his attention toward Rob.

"Do you know who this is?" he yelled, grabbing Rob by the hair and lifting his head off the wall.

Carrie shook her head no, silenced by fear.

"This is my brother."

It didn't take long for Landon and Jake to tire. The mountainside was steep and the ground was unstable, but they were determined to keep climbing.

"Smell that?" Jake asked, pausing to catch his breath.

"Yeah. It's a fire. We must be close. There's a fireplace in the cabin, so someone is in there."

"Yeah," Jake said, wiping the sweat from his face and starting to climb again, "but who?"

Carrie couldn't believe what she had just heard. "You … your brother?"

Proffit's chuckle was spine-tingling. "Oh, that's right," he began mockingly, "you don't know my family's sordid history, do you?"

Carrie shook her head. The pain in her arms was throbbing, sending waves of pain throughout her body. As much as she wanted to concentrate on what this demented man was saying, her focus always fell back to staying awake and applying as much pressure as she could stand alternately to each arm.

Mark and Rob were the sons of Harlan's youngest sister, Reba. Harlan was the eldest of four children, with his brother Gerald and his sister Karen rounding out the bunch.

Reba was the wild child. While Harlen went off and pursued public office, Gerald went to college in Maryland and opened up an architecture business. Karen married a local banker and spent her days raising her children and playing with her grandchildren. Reba was different. She had no plans in life, and moved from boyfriend to boyfriend with no place to call home when the one-night stands ended.

At the age of 19, Reba found herself pregnant with Mark. She was alone, homeless, and scared. She turned to her brothers and sisters for help, and found it in Karen. Karen took Reba in, cared for her, and when it was time to give birth, it was Karen who was there in the delivery room holding Reba's hand; and two weeks later, it was Karen holding Mark when Reba disappeared from town. Karen wasn't ready to be a mother again, especially to a child that wasn't hers, but she had a sense of pride and honor to her family. She couldn't help but care.

In the beginning, Mark's life was wonderful. He lived in a nice house, went to nice schools, and wore nice clothes. What he didn't see was Karen's marriage falling apart because of him. Karen had a difficult choice to make. Her husband had sat her down one night and laid out the ultimatum that would eventually begin the downward spiral in Mark's life. "It's either me or him," her husband had demanded, and she chose her husband.

Though no one wanted to take Mark, the Stanton family was too proud to allow one of their own to wind up in some foster home or orphanage. Throughout his school years, Mark was shuffled from family member to family member with no stability anywhere in his life. The only house he never set foot in was Harlan's. Mark was curious about Harlan and wanted to meet the man he heard so much about. He called the councilman's office for an appointment, and during a lunch meeting with a 16-year-old Mark, Harlan explained that he had no desire to have a child of his own, much less someone else's kid. It was then that the family gave up, swallowed their pride, and placed Mark in foster care.

For the most part, Mark prevailed. He worked hard in school, attended vocational school, and became an auto mechanic, earning more money than many of his cousins. He got himself an apartment and car, and swore that he would never ask his family for anything again. Despite all he felt he owed his family for taking him in, he could not think of another group of people he was angrier at for abandoning him.

Reba made her way to California once she left Mark. She didn't know what she wanted, but she knew whatever it was wouldn't be found in Nashville. She hitchhiked her way across the country, paying for food and motels with her body. She was a beautiful woman with long, light brown hair and brown doe eyes capable of attracting men with a sultry blink. But her rough lifestyle was starting to catch up with her, and she found it difficult to compete with the California beauties and their plastic bodies.

Then she met Wade.

Wade Campbell was a self-made man. A family inheritance left him with the ability to invest in several properties in the Los Angeles suburbs, and by the time he turned 40, he was a millionaire. He had his choice of society's eye candy, but when he saw Reba, it was love at first sight. She was a cashier at a local convenience store and he had stopped in for gas one evening.

It was a whirlwind romance that ended in marriage. Three months later, Reba was pregnant with Rob. Soon, the happy family was on its way to Nashville. Reba was ready to show off her husband, and, most importantly, her money.

Reba and Wade moved into a large house in Brentwood, an elaborate subdivision of Nashville riddled with country music stars' homes, and settled in quite nicely. She and Wade spent her pregnancy spoiling their unborn baby. They set up a nursery furnished with the best that money could buy. Wade treated her like a princess, and considering the hard life she had prior to her marriage, she was eager to be spoiled, too.

Once Rob was born, he lived the easy life. He was able to attend private schools and received an excellent education, while Reba settled into her life of being a rich wife. Everything seemed to be moving along nicely when life threw up a brick wall and Reba ran into it head-first. That wall's name was Mindy.

Mindy was Wade's secretary and she was more breast and sex than work. She was young, leggy, and beautiful. How could Wade not fall in love with her? Reba knew something was up, but chose not to face it until the notice of divorce was handed to her and she collapsed into a ball of tears in the doorway.

Rob was 14 at the time, and he didn't know what to do. His mother slowly turned into depression, then to drugs. She was rarely home, and when she was, she was passed out on the couch until the next junkie came knocking on the door. Rob was afraid, and then he ran to Uncle Harlan who took him in with a smile. Rob had potential, in Harlan's book, and he was more than happy to help out.

Mark abruptly stopped the story. He was obviously getting emotional and turned it into anger and an unconscious Rob bore the brunt of it. Fist after fist struck his already bloody face, spraying drops of blood on the wall and floor, and Carrie couldn't watch anymore. She closed her eyes and begged Mark to stop through a silent prayer.

Suddenly, it was quiet ... the only sound was the fire crackling in the fireplace, a sound that was usually soothing to Carrie, and the heavy breathing of Mark who was obviously worn out from the beating.

"You feel sorry for him, don't you?" He asked.

Carrie opened her eyes. Rob's body was again leaning against the wall, his face swollen and nearly unrecognizable, and Mark was sitting cross-legged on the floor next to him. "I feel sorry for both of you," she whispered.

49

By the time Jake and Landon reached the top of the hill, Jake couldn't breathe and lied on his back trying to catch his breath. Landon snuck up to the house without any restriction. When he reached the porch he remembered the creaking boards, and decided to go to a side window to peer in. Once he saw Carrie, he gasped and ran back to Jake to let him know his sister was in the house and she didn't look good.

Once Rob moved in to Harlan's house, he struggled to adapt. Harlan was a strict disciplinarian who made it clear to Rob that if he didn't like living there, he could certainly move out and move back in with his "whore mother." The words cut Rob to the bone and made him want to shut him up, but he also knew that his mother would want him there, and if he ever wanted to provide a better life for both of them, then he had to stay.

Reba stayed in the Campbell house as they went through the divorce, and when the day came to present their case to the judge, she hired the best lawyer she could find and lost nearly everything when her past came back to haunt her. Within weeks she was out of the house with $15,000 in alimony and back on the street trying to score enough crack to make her forget about everything.

Rob stayed with Harlan and finished high school. Baseball earned him a full ride to the University of Tennessee, where he excelled in sports and academics. Life was going well for the strapping young man who dreamed of a career in engineering. Then the phone call came, not from his family, but from the police.

His mother was dead, her body found in an alley off downtown. It was Rob's final straw.

Rob pawned everything he owned to buy a bus ticket back to Nashville. He grabbed his bag an ran from the bus station across town to Harlan's building. His office building faced town hall and, of course, he was there with his cronies figuring out who to screw next when Rob burst into the conference room, with Harlan's secretary at his heels, stopping all conversation in the room.

Harlan tried to stop his nephew, but it was no good. Rob marched across the room, his fists balled in anger, and before anyone knew what was happening, Harlan was on the floor with a bloody nose, and Rob was standing over him, tears of rage rolling down his cheeks.

The police arrested Rob and he spent the night in jail. Harlan pulled some strings, and refused to press charges.

"That should have been it with them," Mark said. He reached over and grabbed two small twigs from the wood pile next to the fireplace and began snapping them. "I didn't even get a chance to be a part of this family, not for any reason. He walks in and publicly humiliates and injures the almighty Harlan Stanton, and here he is."

"You didn't do all this alone, did you? I mean, all these kidnappings … it couldn't have been just you."

Mark gave her an evil grin. "You are bright. And you are right. I did not do this alone. I had help, and they skipped out on me." He snapped a twig and hurled it into the fire. "And they will pay."

"Who was it?"

Mark smiled again. "Harlan seemed to have a rough time of it, wanting to be a popular, high-powered politician with all of these skeletons in his closet. Of his brother and sister, Karen was the level-headed one, and God help her, she tried to do the right thing. But, Harlan's brother Gerald wasn't as lucky. He was a fine architect, who had a little trouble keeping his pants zipped up. He had two sons with two different women and he never claimed them as his. He paid their mothers some hush money, but when Dane and Brody got old enough to know the truth … well, let's just say they were more than eager to help me out with my little plan to screw the Stanton family."

"So, who did all the dirty work? You?"

Mark laughed. "Oh, honey, you don't know me very well, do you? Flash a few dollars in front of ignorant rednecks and you will get them to do just about anything. Dane was the 'brains' of the operation, but he couldn't handle it. He let a couple of kids get the best of him … can you believe that? A couple of kids…" he shook his head. "When I found that out, I said to just get rid of him. Little did I know that his girlfriend would be so eager to kill him that she shot him dead out there in the forest. That was the best for Brody, anyway, 'cause he and Linda were wanting to get together anyway."

Carrie was about to respond when the reflection of car lights rolled across the dark wall. Mark sprang up to his feet and peered out a window, cussing under his breath. He grabbed Carrie by the arm sending waves of shooting pain through her body and sending her to her knees. In one quick motion Mark picked her up under arms and pulled her to the back of the house; he threw her into a small room and closed the door behind him.

Jake made his way to the cabin. The sound of a car engine and the glow of headlights on the trees concealed his movements. Armed with a large stick he found in the woods in one hand and a small pocketknife in the other, he kicked open the door and waited for a response. There was none except for crackling of the fire and the slight moaning sound coming from Rob's crumpled body. Jake wanted to go check on his new friend, but knew he had to keep focused on who might be in the house.

Landon tugged on Jake's shirt and whispered the layout of the house. To the left of the living room was a hallway that lead to two bedrooms and a non-working bathroom; those were the only places to hide. The crunching of the tires grew closer to the house, and Jake sent the boy to the front window to see who was coming. It was Sheriff Tate.

Jake ran out the door and met the lawman at his car. "Rob's in there on the floor. He's hurt bad from what I can tell. I haven't seen anyone else in there, but I haven't really looked, either."

The sheriff ordered Landon to the patrol car and told him to lock all of the doors and stay out of sight. He then pulled out his cell phone, and sighed. "No signal." He pulled a small pistol out of an ankle holster. "Just stay here and wait."

"No way, dude. I was here first. That's my friend on the floor, and my sister is missing."

"Wait HERE," Tate insisted, turning to look Jake in the eye. "I'll call you in when the coast is clear." He turned and half-walked, half-crawled his way toward the front door.

After identifying himself as law enforcement, he entered the doorway and disappeared into the darkness of the cabin.

Jake leaned against the car and said a silent prayer, something he hadn't done since he was a child. Suddenly he was regretting all of the mean things he had said to his sister in Alabama; the thought of the attitude he gave her brought a knot to his stomach. If anything happened to his sister, he didn't know what he would do. Would he be able to live with the guilt?

Carrie heard the footsteps in the front part of the house, so it was likely thatMark had, too. Her arms were screaming with pain, and fresh blood was quickly working its way through the cloth that covered her injuries. She wanted desperately to scream "HELP!" but feared the wrath she would encounter if she dared make a sound.

Mark was crouched near the door like a tiger ready to pounce on its prey. The knife's blade in his right hand caught glimpses of moonlight, and it was then that she saw the evil reflecting from the blade as it mirrored his face.

The footsteps were slow and unsteady, stopping quite frequently. It wasn't long before they got louder. Whoever it was had reached the hallway and was heading toward Carrie. Mark's grip on the knife tightened as Carrie's heart began to speed up. She slowly sat up on the floor and silently rose to her feet, fighting off the nausea that was making it's was up her throat and caused her head to swim.

The door to the room slowly began to open, and Mark rose, ready to pounce. As he lifted the knife in the air and prepared to strike whoever was on the other side of the door, Carrie thrust herself forward and hit Mark's back with as much force as she could muster. The knife flew through the air and landed behind her as the stunned kidnapper fell through the doorway and landed hard on the floor. Carrie's battered arms took the brunt of her landing and the intense pain quickly knocked her unconscious.

<u>50</u>

Jake couldn't stand the anticipation anymore and slowly made his way into the cabin. The metallic smell of blood was overwhelming. When he turned into the hallway, Sheriff Tate was lying on his back, his eyes closed, with another person lying on his legs. He stepped over the two figures and found Carrie face down on the floor, bloody fabric covering her arms. He ran over to his sister, turned her over, and cradled her in his arms. He sat on the floor and held his sister close, the rhythmic breathing and steady heartbeat comforting him; she was alive.

Sheriff Tate was the first one to make noise, and it was a simple word: "Help." Jake set his sister on the floor gently and made his way to the hallway.

"I think my leg is broken," Tate said through gritted teeth. "Get him off me, please."

Jake picked up the limp body under its arms off the sheriff's legs and placed him to the side. He then helped the sheriff up, and helped him out to the patrol car.

When he returned to the room where Carrie was, his sister was awake and frightened. They embraced, tears soaking each other's shoulders. He picked her up carefully and took her out of the cabin and let her lie on the porch swing. She told him the pain was unbearable, and then turned her attention to the sheriff, letting him know that the man in the hallway was the killer.

A sense of relief encompassed the group as they waited for help to arrive. Sheriff Tate sat on the hood of his car nursing his injured leg. Jake was talking to Landon and Carrie was lying on the swing with her head back, unable to stop her tears from making clean streaks down her dirty cheeks.

The crack of a gunshot came in slow motion. Carrie turned her head to the side and saw the gun, smoke slowly pouring from the barrel. She sat up slowly and followed the end of the barrel and its trajectory with her eyes, and met her brother's eyes. He glanced at her for a moment before a stream of blood began to run out of a small hole just over the left eye.

As Jake's body began to fall backwards, a second shot rang out. Carrie covered her ears and placed her head between her legs, prepared to feel the pain of a bullet entering her body. Landon screamed, and another thud of a body hitting the ground echoed through the trees.

And then there was silence.

The hospital room was cold, freezing almost, the way it had been for days. Carrie sat up in bed and rubbed her bandaged arms. Her wounds were itching, indicating they were healing, but not being able to scratch was driving her crazy.

She put on a pair of grey sweat pants and a blue hoodie, made her way to the elevator, and rode it to the 6th floor. She pushed open the door to the intensive care unit and made her way to room 3.

He was lying there, not asleep, but not awake, either. It hadn't been that way for long. Doctors had wondered if they were even going to be able to save him – head injuries were so unpredictable. Carrie pulled a chair next to the bed and sat, holding his hand. He turned slowly toward her and smiled.

"Hey sweetie," she said, stroking his face gently. "You wanna watch some TV?"

He slowly shook his head, and opened his mouth. He had not spoken since they had arrived. Carrie leaned closer to the bed and heard his whispered words loud and clear; "What happened?"

Epilogue

Mark Proffit was shot and wounded by Sheriff Tate in the doorway of the cabin, but apparently it wasn't enough. Before the sheriff could crawl to the cabin, Mark stumbled back into the dwelling and out the back door. He disappeared into the woods and wasn't seen again.

Local, state, and federal agents convened on the area and searched a 12-mile radius for Mark Proffit, but just like the children that were kidnapped, he just seemed to disappear. Wanted posters were placed in nearly every business in every town in East Tennessee, Western North Caroline, Southwest Virginia, and Northeastern Georgia, but there were no leads. As the posters slowly started to tear or get covered by other notices, the case became cold and Mark Proffit was soon forgotten … at least by some.

Sheriff Tate fully recovered from his injuries, and personally headed the investigation into the kidnappings. Still walking with a limp, he worked the case until it turned cold and the clues quit appearing. Eventually he claimed disability and retired to his home, where he spends his days fishing with his dog, Huber, and spending time with his wife. He and Carrie remained friends and talk every week.

Jake Stevens died on the dirt in front of the cabin that evening. He never regained consciousness. Landon cried over his body, begging him to "wake up," and it took two EMTs and the sheriff to pull the boy away. His voice would haunt Carrie for years.

Jake's body was returned to Alabama and buried in the family cemetery. Though she never got over the loss of her youngest, Carrie and her mother, Debra, became closer than ever, and she was able to convince her mother to move to Tennessee with her. She lives in a small, two-bedroom cabin about 500 feet down the road from Carrie, and the two speak daily.

An investigation later revealed that Landon had escaped the jail by convincing one of the deputies that his toilet was stopped up and he needed to go to the bathroom. The guard took him to the employee's bathroom where the youngster slipped out through a small window.

Deputies discovered the boy's underwear stuffed in the toilet of his cell, causing the bowl to overflow.

Sheriff Mader enjoyed his 15 minutes of fame, but when it was all said and done, he was happy to get back to the slow life in Millersville. The official federal investigation into the kidnappings cites some flaws in Mader's handling of the case, but for the most part, he was praised for his work ethic.

All of the kidnapped children were returned to their parents except one – Thomas. Sheriff Mader located the boy and returned him to his grandmother in Nashville. She says he wasn't the same, and that she was in the process of setting up an appointment with a therapist. One night, he snuck out of the house and disappeared. It was suspected that he returned to Patrick and Luanne in the mountains outside of Millersville, but numerous visits to the home by law enforcement officials showed no sign of the boy. One month later, the couple moved to Oregon.

Johnson Pickering was found loitering outside a bar in downtown Nashville. The teen was angry at his parents, just as Rob had suspected, and ran away. He was returned to his mother, but ran away again within days. Rumor has it that he was eventually sent away to a private military school.

Robert Holton left that cabin on a stretcher, clinging to life. He would require numerous surgeries to repair the broken bones and brain injuries suffered at the hands of his brother. Harlan never came to visit him at the hospital, but an envelope with the remaining money due him was found on a table next to his hospital bed one morning. He is still recovering from his injuries, and Carrie is right there by his side every day helping in any way she can.

Harlan Stanton left office within days. Though an investigation later revealed he had nothing to do with his nephew's actions, the public didn't buy it, and demanded he be removed. Days of picketing, e-mails, and death threats were more than the councilman could take, and late one night, he cleared out his office and disappeared.

His name was soon forgotten in Davidson County, but his love of public office continued, and he was later found to be running for city council in a small town in Texas. He lost.

Miranda and Willie Tyler were returned to their councilman father Billy, without a scratch on them. Billy was the first parent to show up in Millersville to collect his children, and was the last to leave. He personally thanked everyone that helped with the investigation, and was appointed chairman of the City Council in the wake of Harlan's resignation.

Charlie was cleared in the disappearance of the children, and the cause of the blood in the car is still unsolved.

Carrie Stevens' right arm was shattered either from the fall in the house or from the powerful knife blows she sustained. She never regained feeling in her left forearm or hand and had to undergo several surgeries to repair the damage. She, too, received the remaining money due her in an envelope in her room.

Carrie was offered her job back at the *Nashville News*, but she decided to leave her options open. She took her money and bought a house on the outskirts of Rugby, Tenn., where she lives with her cat, Charlie, Rob, and their two children, Jake and Tammy.

A quick shake of the head brought Carrie back to reality. She walked back into the house, poured a fresh cup of coffee, and walked back to her office. She had been working on her book for a year, and as it was nearing its end, Carrie found the memories were becoming harder and harder to endure. She rubbed her scars once again, and sat behind her computer, ready to finish the story once and for all.

A sound from the driveway drew her attention, and by the time she made it to the door, whatever had caused the sound was gone. She was about to close the front door when a flash of white on the welcome mat caught her eye. She looked down and picked up a shoebox with a sealed envelope with her name scrawled on the outside of it taped to the lid.

Carrie slid her finger under the flap and opened the envelope. Inside was a note that simply read "ready for Act II?" When she opened the shoebox lid, its contents made her scream and drop the box on the floor as she ran upstairs to get Rob.

In the doorway lay the bloody pocketknife and a twig.

Made in the USA
San Bernardino, CA
24 February 2018